PRESENT TENSE

GIL HOGG

PRESENT TENSE

A story of rape and revenge

Matador
5 Weir Road
Kibworth Beauchamp
Leicester LE8 0LQ, UK
Tel: (+44) 116 279 2299
Fax: (+44) 116 279 2277
Email: books@troubador.co.uk
Web: www.troubador.co.uk/matador

ISBN 978 1848 764 262

British Library Cataloguing in Publication Data.
A catalogue record for this book is available from the British Library.

Typeset in 11pt Bembo by Troubador Publishing Ltd, Leicester, UK

Matador is an imprint of Troubador Publishing Ltd

Printed in Great Britain by the MPG Books Group, Bodmin and King's Lynn

BY THE SAME AUTHOR

FICTION

A Smell of Fraud

The Predators

Caring for Cathy

Blue Lantern

NON-FICTION

Teaching Yourself Tranquillity

1

The first sight I had of him in fifteen years was that moment, in the crowd, at the bar of the Abbott's Point Golf Club, Monroe County, in upper New York State. He was half turned towards me. I could see his short, red-gold hair, ruddy cheeks, and the thick neck of a college quarterback.

I hadn't the slightest doubt. The man was Dwight Chadwin.

I was shocked. I disengaged from the people around me. I put out my hand, rested the glass of wine I had been drinking on a shelf, and steadied myself with my fingertips touching the wall.

I looked across the room for my husband. Greg had just come into the clubhouse with his buddies. He was over the other side of the bar, settling bets after the game. We had arranged that morning that we would meet at the club, have a few drinks with friends, and go home early together.

My eyes were drawn back to the man at the bar. Yes, it was Chadwin. A few pounds heavier now, but in good shape under a navy-blue jacket; a flat belly, narrow waist, and with his jutting jaw nodding agreeably to his audience.

I had difficulty in drawing breath. I made a move to cross the room toward Greg. At the same time, the people around Chadwin parted, and blocked my way. Marty Kutash, Greg's boss, with a friendly hand on Chadwin's arm, stepped forward.

"Loren, I'd like you to meet Bucky Chadwin, a new member, from Pittsburgh."

I felt like running. I couldn't manage a 'Hello,' and inclined my head a little.

Marty turned to Chadwin. "Loren is Greg Stamford's wife. You remember meeting Greg?"

Chadwin surged forward. His golden-haired paw reached out for my hand which was dead at my side, and his pale, blue-tinted eyes cascaded down my body.

"I'm very pleased to meet you, Loren," he said, warmly.

I never spoke. My eyes flickered as they met his. It wasn't embarrassment or shame or fear. I had simply lost control of my reactions for a moment. Chadwin had a sociable smile. Nothing disturbed his pudgy, self-confident features. He did not give the slightest sign of recognition.

I stepped back when Chadwin let go of my hand, tripped on the edge of a rug, and nearly fell. Chadwin's attention was diverted to somebody else. The crowd closed around him, shutting me out. My fear had been that I must be as recognisable to him, as he was to me. Instead, and thankfully, I seemed to be no more than the unknown wife of another club member.

"You OK, Loren?" Marty Kutash asked, taking my arm. "You look pale, kid."

"I have a migraine. I'm going to ask Greg to take me home."

Greg was his usual agreeable self when I said I wanted to leave so promptly, though perhaps he gunned the car out of the parking lot more briskly than usual.

"I'd have liked to stay longer," he said, eventually, in the silence when we were on the road.

"I'm sorry. It's only a company party."

Greg glanced quickly at me, frowning, trying to get my mood. "We have to earn our living."

"Not at the bar at Abbott's Point," I said, knowing I was being unfair.

"Joining was your idea, my dear."

I barely listened, as Greg reminded me, lightly, that I had pointed out to him years before the importance of the social side of business. I felt ill as the car rolled softly on the curves of the Medford Parkway, its tyres moaning.

"Could you slow down, please?" I asked.

Greg spared me another quick look. Then he eased up, both the speed of the car, and his manner. "OK, I'm being a pig. But I should have got around a bit more tonight. As one of the membership committee, I have to take an interest in the new members, Loren."

"Chadwin?"

"Amongst others. Did you meet Mrs Chadwin?"

"No."

There had to be a Mrs Chadwin. Probably more than one in the past as well.

"Donna introduced me. You'd like her. She owns a slice of Hudson," Greg said.

Hudson Electronics, Chadwin's new employer, was one of the big companies in the Chester Forks area.

"One way to get her husband a job."

"I don't think so, Loren. Chadwin will have to deliver."

I sighed. I was trying to think of a way to bring the conversation to a point where I could open my concerns to Greg. It had seemed unnecessary to tell Greg when I met him ten years ago, and every year since had confirmed how unnecessary it was – until now.

I looked out of the car at the blue satin sky over the hedges and rooftops of Park Drive. As Greg turned the car into our driveway, the beech on the lawn fluttered its copper leaves against the whiteness of the house. The lights were on, and I could see through the conservatory, deep inside the living room. I had a sense of a bright and beating heart of security in there. Roseanne, from next door, who baby-sat for us, would be struggling to get the girls washed up. My sister Grace would be waiting in the girls' bedroom to read them a story.

Our home on Park Drive was the centre of everything that was important in my life. It seemed to me to be solid, untouchable. The house was in the Cedar Falls area of Monroe County. Cedar Falls was quiet, with wide, well sealed roads, and family houses set in spacious lawns and gardens. The neighbourhood was middle class, business and professional people. I would concede that it was an ordinary, somewhat dull, and rather predictable place.

Greg and I owned a three level wooden frame house, set well back from the road in an acre of ground. You find a similar kind of house in many parts of middle America, with verandahs, a mansard roof and a variety of spacious rooms. I had always thought that the outside suggested that the inside must be comfortable. We had lived in Park Drive for five years. With Greg and the children, it was more than I ever seriously thought I would have.

Chadwin didn't quite invade my life in those few seconds at the clubhouse bar. I already had a painful inkling of what I feared, earlier today, at breakfast. I heard the name 'Chadwin,' whispered as it were, out of the darkness of the past. Greg had come downstairs. He was a slim, five feet eleven inches, with a frizz of thin, dry, fair hair, and a long face with good-humoured lines around the eyes and mouth. He was dressed for the office, swinging his light grey suit jacket over his shoulder. He pressed his lips to my cheek in a preoccupied way.

Greg wasn't a worrier, but he was always brisk on Monday mornings. Instead of sitting at the breakfast bar, where I had placed half a grapefruit and a bowl of cereal, he picked up the diary by the phone. He was going to mention the schedule for the week. I was distracted for a moment by the noise from the girls upstairs. They were yelling at each other and my sister Grace. I decided the commotion didn't require me to go to the rescue, but I wasn't quite listening to Greg. When I focussed on what he was actually saying, a few words loomed up out of all the rest.

"We'll be meeting the Chadwins at the golf club tonight."

I thought I had misheard. "Who?"

"The Chadwins. Loren, listen, please. By the way, you're spilling the orange juice."

I looked at the mess I had made on the bench. I said I'd meet Greg at Abbott's Point at six, and asked again about the people we'd be meeting.

"A new member and his wife. He's joining Hudson. I wasn't at the membership meeting. I don't know much more. He's being fast-tracked."

Being fast-tracked meant that this particular Chadwin was jumping a two or three year queue to join the club. It meant that he had influence. When Greg had finished his breakfast, he came over to me. I was stacking the dishwasher. He put his arms around my waist from behind.

"You're not yourself this morning, honey. Didn't you sleep?"

Before I could answer, Gail screamed from upstairs, and there was a heavy crash.

"I'll have to go and see what's happening," I said, unwrapping myself from Greg, and heading for the stairs.

"OK, babe. See you at Abbott's Point," he said, slipping on his jacket, and going through to the garage.

Fifteen minutes after Greg had left for the office, I was sitting behind the wheel of the Jeep 4WD in the drive. We bought the Jeep for our visits to our house at Lake Chateaugay, to tow the sailboat trailer. The engine was idling. Gail and Rosemary were loading parcels of costumes, made from old clothes of mine, which they were taking to school for a play. On Mondays, the twins had a preschool gym class, and I had the time to drive them to Mt Vernon School, and make my office by nine. I was watching the progress of the pair in the rear-view mirror.

"Hurry up! You'll be late for the gym," I said, but without any real urgency.

Close up – in the rear-view mirror – I thought I looked healthful. Clear, unlined skin. My shoulder length hair had a natural wave, and a natural golden-blonde colour. I was wearing a tweed skirt and jacket, with a blouse tied at the throat, and little makeup. My dress was unfussy. I didn't spend a lot of time on grooming.

I leaned back on the head-rest, and closed my eyes. I wasn't tired, as Greg had suggested at breakfast. In my mind, there was a dark spot which spoiled the pleasure of the Monday morning flurry in the house. I enjoyed getting the children ready for school. I was always slightly amused by Greg's beginning-of-the-week sharpness which so contrasted with his laid-back weekend self. I liked the thought of a challenging week at the office. And there was always the agreeable anticipation of little engagements during the week, a keep-fit class, shopping for a present for Greg's forty-first birthday... All these events were suddenly shaded.

If I opened my eyes slightly, I could see an imperfection in my image in the mirror. My nose was very slightly thickened at the bridge. It was a small irregularity which Greg insisted gave me character, but I wasn't really convinced. Every time I looked at my face in the mirror, and turned my head slightly, I could see that one side of my face wasn't quite the same as the other. Over the years, I had made myself ignore it, and one of the ways of doing this was to spend as little time as possible looking at myself. That's why I didn't bother too much with makeup.

At this time, on the morning of the meeting at Abbott's point, I was telling myself that I was being stupid. We were going to meet a couple named Chadwin. So? There were probably hundreds, or thousands of Chadwins in America. It wasn't a common name, but surely it wasn't all that uncommon. My life was just as good at this moment, sitting in the Jeep, as it had been when I slipped out from under Greg's warm arm in bed, an hour or so earlier. I was foolish to succumb to mere pulses of alarm flicking through my mind.

I felt a gentle touch on my cheek, and opened my eyes fully. It was Gail's hand.

"I thought you were in a hurry, Mom," she said.

"This isn't the time to sleep," Rosemary added, as I made a startled flurry to ensure the children were secure, clicked my seatbelt, and rolled the car down the drive.

I saw my sister Grace at the dining room window as we passed, watching with a self-contained smile. Grace waved and the children waved back.

"I got sleepy waiting for you two," I said to the girls, feeling defensive.

"That's funny because we've been sitting in the back, waiting for you for the last minute or so," Rosemary said.

At the gate, I swung the Jeep to the right, to go up Park Drive to Mt Vernon. My gaze fanned the empty, tree-lined road, with its neatly clipped verges as I eased the vehicle forward.

Gail gave a high-pitched scream. I stomped the brake, and froze.

With a deafening horn blast, and a yowl of tyres, a black Cadillac sedan swung wide past us. I hadn't seen it! It had appeared from nowhere!

"Gee, that was close!" Gail giggled now.

"Mom, you really are asleep this morning. Admit it!" Rosemary said.

I set the children down at Mt Vernon School with their bags, and greeted Mr Pegler the duty teacher who saw all the pupils safely inside the gate. Then I drove the four miles to the Ulex Business Machines site, on a new industrial park a few miles outside Rochester. The park was landscaped with rolling green lawns, and high-tech glass buildings. I usually got a pleasurable buzz out of arriving on a Monday, knowing that an airy, pastel-coloured office awaited me, with my own personal-assistant, and a pile of work that I was beginning to handle with increased confidence. But I didn't get a kick this morning. I gave and received greetings from others, as I strolled from the parking lot to the office buildings. I was one of the senior people in the finance department, well-known and, I believe, well-liked. I acknowledged my colleagues with a mechanical wave of my arm. The dark spot was still there.

When I reached my office, I spent a few moments chatting to Sally, my PA, pleasantries about the weekend. I asked for coffee. I went into my room, logged on to the computer and checked my diary. Monday morning was usually spent in the office, preparing for the meetings of the rest of the week. It was a relief to see the task list for the day. Nothing I couldn't put off.

I sat at my desk with the coffee, staring at the screen. I dealt with reports from staff, answered Sally's queries, and the phone. The morning passed in a haze. At twelve-thirty I left the office.

Chesterfield, population 6,800, was the town nearest to Cedar Falls, and most of the residents of Cedar Falls regarded it as 'their' town, rather than Chester Forks, which was further down the Caribou River, much bigger, and industrialised.

The town was on the south bank, overlooking the river. It had a grassed town square – actually a triangle – with benches shaded by maples and oaks. The main shops, the courthouse, two churches, and the sheriff's office surrounded the Square. Chesterfield, originally a farming centre, had become an attractive retirement place over the years. The shops had moved stealthily up-market. Three were selling antiques. There were two fine art galleries, an antiquarian bookshop, and a collection of exclusive boutiques.

It was after 1pm. I didn't feel hungry, and was thinking about getting back to the office. I was coming out of James & Charles, the men's shop on the Square. I had wandered through the store, feeling silk ties, looking at the tooling on waist-belts, trying to think of a present for Greg. I couldn't concentrate, and without deciding anything, I drifted out of the door.

"Loren, honey. Hi!" a drawly voice greeted me.

I looked up to see Donna Kutash in very high heels, and a long, clipped mink coat to keep out the chill that was creeping into the air.

"Hi, Donna. I was dreaming."

"How about a little something?"

"I have to get back."

Donna's husband, Marty, was a managing director at Insel, another of the big local corporations. Greg, who was head of corporate planning, reported to him. I therefore had to view Donna and Marty as compulsory friends. I relented.

We linked arms and went into Giovanni's Coffee Shop. Donna could never resist the homemade strawberry cheesecake when she was in town. We found a table. I had a cappuccino, while I watched Donna fork the rich, scarlet mix into her mouth.

We talked about Marty's team's hopes in the golf tournament. Greg was a team member. Donna wiped the cream from her full lips. I mentioned the new members. I couldn't get my mouth around the name Chadwin.

"Oh, yeah," Donna said, chasing the last fragment of strawberry and cake on her plate with her fork, and finally blocking it with a long, polished fingernail, "the Chadwins. She's a together lady, but OK. I met her at Kitty Calino's. Loaded, I'm told. From LA, I think."

The mention of Los Angeles was a sudden relief. LA was a world away. I brightened. There were thousands of Chadwins in America!

My state of mind at lunchtime on Monday was relieved, hopeful. I put in a zombie-like attendance at the office in the afternoon, and went home at 5pm to change. I wouldn't normally have bothered to go home before going to the club. It was not so much that I wanted to have a shower and change my clothes; I wanted to take myself apart metaphorically, and reassemble the pieces. The twins were clattering around the house, and Grace was trying to organise them. Gail, always the most timid, came into the bedroom and watched me silently as I moved around in my bra and pants.

"You all right now, Mom?" she asked, finally.

"Of course I'm fine! Don't stand there staring at me, please. Go and get a cookie from the kitchen. Only one."

Rosemary, the shrewd one, appeared to replace her sister, her head leaning against the door frame. "Why are you dithering about, Mom?"

I sank onto the bed, my hands in my lap, my eyes on the copper beech on the lawn, riffling in the wind. I reasoned that even if Chadwin was *the* Chadwin, he was now a mature man with an influential wife and a responsible job. What could I ever have to fear from such a person?

"I'm not dithering," I said, as resolutely as I could.

"Really?" Rosemary said, raising her eyebrows and poking out her tongue in disbelief.

This was how I stumbled forward to that meeting at the Abbott's Point clubhouse.

2

That night after seeing Chadwin again, I untangled myself from Greg in our bed, and lay rigid, remembering events that I never ever wanted to recall.

Fifteen years had passed since the stiflingly hot summer day when I was a witness at the Westchester County Court, at Yonkers, New York for the prosecution of Dwight Chadwin and Duane Schultz, on charges of forcible rape and assault.

I went to court that day thinking that this would be an end of the pain, and I could start forgetting. My sister Grace, aged eighteen, wasn't in court. She was a patient in a psychiatric hospital. I hadn't fared so badly as my sister. I still had a brace on my neck to keep my jaw-line straight. The bandages were not long off my nose and left cheek. The deep bruising was going, leaving a yellow stain which the doctor said would go too, eventually. But my nose would never be the same. The bone, and the cartilage in the bridge had been smashed, and there were medical difficulties in setting my broken jaw.

After I had known Greg for a while, he took my head in his hands one day, and said my face was beautifully irregular. I told him I'd been in a car crash. I was clear in my mind that it wouldn't help to tell Greg about Chadwin *then*. I didn't rule out ever telling him. I just didn't want to pollute a pure and decent and loving relationship with a vile event of the past. And I certainly hoped that the need to tell would never arise.

It's probably not surprising that Chadwin didn't recognise me at Abbott's Point. The face of a woman in her mid thirties, compared to the face of a nineteen-year-old girl he saw for perhaps half an hour, and then wearing a neck-brace in court, all those years ago.

I remember that the corridors of the court building smelled with the sourness of sweaty, depressed people. They moved woodenly, enclosed in their separate veils of worry. My persistent enquiries from officials located Mr Bronstein, the Assistant District Attorney who was going to try the case. I knocked at the door of counsel's room, and eventually he came out, blinking.

"Ah, yes, Miss Reynaud," he said, trying at first I think, to fit me into his crowded morning.

Then he examined me with a penetrating look. "How are your injuries...?"

"Nearly better. I'll soon have this thing off."

He took me to an interview room, windowless, with brown stained walls, and a flickering fluorescent light. He was intense and nervy. He had bitten fingernails, and a low, sensitive voice.

"Look, Miss Reynaud," he said, without any preliminaries, other than to point to a chair. "I've been reviewing the evidence, and talking to counsel for Chadwin and Schultz."

He paused, held my stare with his watery eyes, and I got the idea that he was preparing me for something, not actually asking my approval, but wanting it.

"We can get a guilty plea to assault, but if we press the rape charges, it's going to be a full trial in front of a jury, and you're going to get a hard time under cross-examination."

"I don't mind that. I can only tell what happened."

"It's an ordeal, Miss Reynaud, believe me."

"It can't be worse than I've been through!"

Bronstein was in his early thirties. Hard work showed in the permanent furrows in his brow, and his skin pallor. Thin black hair straggled across his scalp. I suppose he had tried a lot of cases. His sympathy for me was swamped by his cynical knowledge of court procedures. He gave me a sincere look that seemed genuine, and sat down in the chair beside me.

"It's an ordeal of a different kind, Miss Reynaud," he said, gesturing feebly to try to cover so much that was too complicated to explain, and glancing at the clock on the wall. "The lawyers for the accused men are very sharp..."

"Are you afraid of them?"

"I can't stop them taking you apart, Miss Reynaud," he said stiffening.

"Let them try."

"They may look like your daddy..."

"My father's an unemployed auto-worker."

Bronstein sighed and thumbed his file distastefully. "What I'm saying, Miss Reynaud, is that I can't get convictions for rape. The evidence isn't there. And I don't want to put you through an ordeal."

"I don't understand what you're saying Mr Bronstein. One guy raped Grace. The other raped me. And they beat us up!"

Art Bronstein looked at the clock again. He was in a hurry. He now seemed to have half a mind on me. He mumbled something about other witnesses to see. He looked uncomfortable, as though he had indigestion.

"I know, and I believe you. I think it's a terrible case. But I have to prove it. Your word alone won't do it."

"The doctor said it was rape."

"No, he did not," Bronstein said, shaking his head sorrowfully. "The doctor confirms that you and your sister had bruising and abrasions in the area of the vagina, and that you were sexually penetrated very roughly."

"Isn't that enough?" I asked, incredulously.

"No, Miss Reynaud, it isn't. The doctor will have to admit, if pressed, and he will be, that the injuries could be consistent with the kind of struggling which happens between consenting parties."

"Mr Bronstein that is … complete rubbish!" I said, crying now.

Bronstein nodded sagely, a man who had been through a version of this dialogue more than once.

"Let me tell you, Miss Reynaud, that many young women get injuries similar to these because they neck for hours on a park bench, or in the back of a car, performing contortions in awkward places, wrestling with belts and buckles and tight clothing, and eventually consent to sexual intercourse."

"Chadwin raped me. And Shultz raped Grace, and she couldn't say a word!"

Bronstein went on evenly. "And some people have sex roughly, when the woman isn't lubricated, and there may be medical evidence of internal abrasions, but it doesn't necessarily amount to evidence of rape."

"What are you going to do?" I asked, feeling the wet lines down my cheeks.

Bronstein patted my arm encouragingly. "I understand. I believe you, but…"

"What about Grace?"

Bronstein riffled his papers to find Grace. "She's part of the problem. We need her evidence. She hasn't been able to make a statement. May be in hospital indefinitely."

"But what do you expect, Mr Bronstein? She's been frightened nearly to death!"

Bronstein traced the lines of a report with the chewed fingernail of a thick, white forefinger. "Your sister's mental condition is documented before the incident."

"She's autistic. This punk put her in hospital."

"I realise that, but the law doesn't presume your sister is in hospital because of what Schultz did to her. She was already a sick girl."

"Surely it's obvious after what she went through."

"Not to the law," Bronstein said, mildly.

"What's the law for, if not to protect people like Grace?"

Bronstein ignored me and pressed on. "Grace isn't in hospital because of her physical abrasions. We can't tell whether her mental condition is a result of what Schultz did to her. The doctors can't say. She can't talk to us."

"God! It's plain!"

There was a long pause. Bronstein looked at me apologetically, his upper lip damp, and the growth of blue-black hairs on his hastily shaven cheeks casting his face in shadow. I could see it was no use pursuing my argument.

Bronstein said he would arrange for a guilty plea on the assault charges. "Chadwin and Schultz will go inside for six months, something like that. I mean, the serious facts will come out in court, Miss Reynaud."

It seemed wrong to me but I knew nothing of the workings of the law. Bronstein looked hard at me, willing my agreement.

"No."

"Whaddya mean?" Bronstein frowned.

"I think the case should be heard by the jury."

Bronstein's intelligent hazel eyes showed understanding – how an ignorant kid of nineteen had the nerve to say this. Then he brushed his palm over his scalp, and pulled himself back to his morning's work. He sneaked another look at the clock.

"Whatsamatter?" he demanded loudly, the brotherly manner slipping away. "Six months in the pen not enough?"

"I wasn't thinking of that."

"You want vengeance?" he asked, accusingly.

"I want it to come out in court like it happened."

A cop in shirtsleeves came in with a note for Bronstein, and he stood up to go. He read the note, and turned to me, preoccupied.

"Like it happened?" he echoed.

"Yes. I want to tell the judge."

Bronstein moved to the door in his crumpled, shiny suit, the file jammed under his arm. He was on another case now, another problem, and the intimacy of our talk had gone.

He turned back at the door, detached. "Yeah, that's what everybody wants. Like it happened. But no can do. This is a court, Miss Reynaud, not a replay of a real life video. All we have is evidence. Evidence is never like it happened. Never."

I was in Court 2 when the People versus Chadwin and Schultz was called, hours later.

The defendants were summoned to the dock, two very innocent young-looking men, in neat ties and dark suits, with white shirts, their hair plastered down.

Rows of people sat in front of me, hunched and uneasy on hard seats. The room was dark-panelled and gloomy, the temperature over eighty. Moisture trickled under my arms. The air was stale with disappointment. On the bench a wrinkled old man in a gown, flapped like a black bat.

The judge called counsel to approach him. Bronstein went forward, showing the bagginess of his suit, and the bald spot at the back of his head. The two defence attorneys had sleekly draped suits, and barbered layers of dark grey hair. The lawyers huddled with the judge like birds pecking at crumbs.

When counsel returned to their seats, the judge announced that the cases would be dealt with together, on guilty pleas to assault. It was like a case which didn't involve me and my sister. The judge said he was grateful to counsel for saving the court's time, and he would hear counsel in mitigation, and give sentence.

Bronstein stood up and gave a fluent outline of facts which I hardly recognised; it was neutral, uncritical, devoid of interpretation. Two girls had been picked up by the defendants in a car, and taken to a place where sexual intercourse had occurred between the girls and the defendants. The parties had argued, and consumed alcoholic liquor, and each of the girls had been assaulted. Bronstein detailed the injuries. In my case a broken jaw, and bruising to my face and vagina. Grace had bruising to her breasts and vagina. He said she had not yet been discharged from hospital, but was suffering from a pre-existing psychiatric disorder. Bronstein's clinical words made the event sound unimportant and ordinary.

After Bronstein, Chadwin's lawyer spoke. He conjured up a scene which made you think you were in a scented garden, instead of a smelly court. He spoke of Chadwin's family, how community minded they were, perfect American citizens. And Bucky, what a credit he was to them; president of his class at Maplehurst College, one of the best collegiate footballers of his day, destined in future without doubt to graduate Phi Beta Kappa from Columbia University.

When the lawyer referred to what happened on that fateful Saturday afternoon, he might have been talking about two women whom I didn't know. Two clean-living and attractive young men made the mistake of giving two hitchiking girls from Tarrytown a ride. He implied that the girls were undiscriminating about who picked them up, and did this for fun. The men were not used to dealing with girls of this background. The lawyer put this gross proposition so delicately, that it seemed perfectly understandable. The men were innocents who were placed at a disadvantage. They concluded quite reasonably that the girls were willing to have intercourse. They all shared some drink which the girls showed a readiness to consume. The men were encouraged.

What followed, the lawyer said, was deeply regretted by Chadwin. It was a momentary loss of self control which was unforgivable, but understandable. His client had lost his temper when Loren Reynaud, who was drunk, bit his tongue.

I rose slowly to my feet to protest that there were so many lies, but my voice was dry in my throat. The people behind were muttering at me to sit down. The police orderly came down the aisle, gesturing at me to sit, or leave. I sank back on the seat.

The other lawyer followed in the same vein. You would have thought that Duane Schultz was preparing to take holy vows. He had intercourse with Grace Reynaud with her full consent, and when the argument between Chadwin and her sister occurred, Grace had become aggressive. All Schultz was doing was to defend himself against her, and he had no intention of using force that bruised her breasts. He very much regretted what he had done. The lawyer was very careful to emphasise that Grace had seemed to Schultz to be in every respect a perfectly healthy girl. Shultz couldn't be held in the slightest way responsible for the disability which kept her in hospital.

The speeches shook me. I felt like shouting out, but my head was a jumble of words. What was being said was so unbelievably distorted and wrong.

When the judge began his sentencing speech I realized, with relief, that he was angry. His eyes were wide and accusatory in his dark face. He had seen through the fine words! He had experience. He saw it from a different angle.

"You behaved like wild brutes!" he said in a raised voice to Chadwin and Schultz. "You cruelly beat up two young women whom you should have respected and protected. It doesn't matter what part of town they come from!"

Chadwin and Schultz were buffeted by the storm of words as they faced the judge. The atmosphere of an unfortunate, boyish incident, which their lawyers had created, had vanished. The smirky dimples at the corners of their mouths had been replaced by gritted teeth.

I brought my mind back to what the judge was actually saying. Now, suddenly, he had changed his tone. The wrinkled old man on the bench had switched from savagery to benevolence, like an actor auditioning for a part, one moment fierce and threatening, the next wise and generous. It was as though he had thought it was necessary to scare Chadwin and Shultz, or give the journalists a headline for the local papers, and that was all done now.

"I have to take into account your clean records, the excellent family backgrounds you both have, and your promising future, which leads me to conclude that you won't offend again," he said, with a slight smile.

"I have to note that the young women went with you willingly, in circumstances where you had grounds to assume that they were prepared to have sexual intercourse..."

"No!" I shouted.

I couldn't control myself. The pile of untruths had mounted so high.

"Quiet!" the court orderly said in a ringing tone.

"It's not true!" I said, standing up as a meaty, bare-armed police officer advanced aggressively down the aisle towards me.

People turned round and stared at me, a girl with a neck brace on. The judge continued his soft speech, taking no notice.

"The young women had been drinking, and that must cast confusion over their words and actions..."

"It's a lie! A lie!"

The police officer pushed the people near me aside, dug his fingers into my arm, and hauled me bodily into the aisle.

"You wanna contempt charge?" he hissed.

The officer jostled me to the back of the court, by the swing doors.

"I should send you both to be locked away," the judge was saying in a deeper tone, reverting for a moment to his irate citizen pose.

"Let me hear this please," I begged the cop.

The judge growled on in a monotone. "But in the circumstances, I'll suspend conviction and sentence, subject to you both being placed under strict supervision for six months on a community service programme. In addition you are each ordered to pay a two thousand dollar contribution to the costs of the case. If you don't comply with the conditions of the programme you'll return to this court, and I'll enter convictions and sentence."

"No!" I yelled, and the cop opened the doors, and pushed me into the hall.

I was almost fainting in the crowded hall when Bronstein found me. He placed a warm hand on my shoulder, and pleaded with me to try to understand. His voice was gentle, full of real sympathy.

"The case has been dealt with now. It's over. Go home Miss Reynaud, and try to forget."

"All over?" I choked, my chin sticking in the neck brace.

Bronstein rubbed his forehead uncertainly. "Look, I didn't think the old man would impose community service. I think he completely misjudged it..."

Just then, Chadwin and the others, the lawyers, parents, brothers and sisters, came sweeping through the doorway from the court, their heads up, disdainful of the grubby crowd which loitered in the hall. Two young men with their hands in their pockets slouched behind the rest, satisfaction smeared across their baby-smooth faces. The phalanx went past me looking straight ahead, as though they could discern the pleasurable future which lay before them, and I guessed they could.

I felt bitterly ashamed and soiled.

3

I don't think I slept at all the night we came home from the golf club party. I was left at dawn with the ache of a memory dismissed so long from the front of my mind. As the beech trees swayed in the breeze outside our bedroom window, I saw a vision of Chadwin as he was now, at the Abbott's Point bar, the businessman, rocking his shoulders as he talked, strutting amongst his new acquaintances, every move saying, 'Aren't I great?'

On that Tuesday morning it wasn't easy with Greg and the girls. The three of them whispered together that Mom was in a bad mood, and they better keep out of the way. I was glad they left me alone.

After breakfast, when Grace and the children had left the table, I said I might drive up to our summer house at Lake Chateaugay, near the Keuka State Park in York County, on Friday, after work, and start getting the place ready for winter.

"I need some time on my own," I added, before Greg could offer to help.

"What's the matter?"

I tried to tell him, wanted to tell him, but my voice was still, and my lips closed. I had rehearsed every word of an explanation in the night, but I couldn't speak. The impact on Greg would be heavy, and I feared its effects. I had the perhaps absurd hope, that if I didn't tell, Chadwin would have less substance, be less real. Yes, Chadwin was here physically, and we had met momentarily, but maybe we would never need to meet again. If I told Greg, he'd be understanding and protective; that was his nature. But he'd be deeply upset, angry with Chadwin, and hurt that I had not shared my secret. Bringing it all into the open would mean making Greg as unhappy and anxious as I was. Although it was a delicate balance, because sharing with Greg would make it much easier for me. I decided I could handle the problem alone. I've always believed in my right, if you like, to silence over some events in my life; and that goes with an inclination to solve my own problems, rather than collapse on the shoulder of my husband or friends.

"I feel a bit down. I'll be OK."

"Anything I've done? Or the kids?"

"No. It's work."

I knew I could be starting to dig myself into a hole, but I couldn't help it.

"Well, you have a big job. I'm not surprised it gets you down at times. How long will you be away?"

"There's a lot to do. Sunday afternoon."

"Are you going to take Grace? She'd be a big help."

"She's got a class on Saturday morning."

Later, when Greg had gone to the office, and Grace was preparing to take the children to school, I saw her watching me carefully. She usually said little, but was sensitive to my moods.

"What's troubling you, Loren? I haven't seen you like this for ages."

"Office politics, honey. The zoo is too much at times."

I did not want Grace at Chateaugay. I wanted time and a place to think. Although Grace didn't talk much, and was never inquisitive, we were very close. What was troubling me would disturb Grace, and eventually, if we were alone I would have to tell her.

I have always lived with Grace. Greg has accepted her as part of the family without demur. She was a pleasant but withdrawn person, whose role was somewhere between housekeeper, cook and child-minder. Grace was diagnosed as autistic when she was a child, but I believed she had never fully recovered from the rape and assault by Schultz. Greg knew that she had suffered an awful experience with a man years ago, but we never talked about the precise details.

After I had blamed my dejection on my problems at the office, we had a superficially calm but uneasy week at home. I tried hard to prevent it, but my concern communicated itself to Greg and Grace like a virus. I was glad when Saturday came.

I arranged with Rosanne, our babysitter, to give Greg and Grace extra help with the girls, and drove the Jeep up to Chateaugay on Saturday morning. The hundred and some miles along the Eastern Expressway, Interstate 90, and Route 6 to Clayburg, passed easily in what was like summer rather than autumn weather. I had a Van Morrison compact disc on the stereo. I was looking for the bright side of the road.

At Clayburg I turned off toward Guyanoga. Our place, 'Pine Hill', is in a forest of black pine, spruce and beech, beside the lake, a dozen miles beyond the town. I drove the car off the lake road, onto the concrete forecourt beside the house. The land rises here, and the house is on a high point, with a view over the forest to the south, and over the lake to the north. At ground level, the whole width of the building is a garage and storeroom-workshop. Above, there are four big bedrooms, and beyond them, with a view over the lake, are the living rooms. We have a jetty on the lake, and a ramp to launch our boats. The only houses in sight are miles away, across the water.

Chateaugay is a beautiful place, and it never takes me long to respond to the soughing of the trees, and the sight of chipmunks and squirrels and bluejays and robins. But I wasn't responding today. I left the car in front of the garage, and went up the steps to the door. I unlocked it and went inside, disturbing a silence which still contained the carefree sounds of the children, as they echoed through the rooms a few weeks ago. The place had a chill.

In the kitchen, I switched on the central heating, made a cup of powdered coffee, and sat in my favourite thinking place, the diner, by the window, looking across the lawn toward the road. I could see the flowerbeds, with wind-burned late roses, the trees swaying in the wind, and beyond, a sparkling sliver of Lake Chateaugay. I was thinking that life for the Stamfords was very good, and I had to aim for some sort of detachment from the black cloud which inevitably swelled in my memory.

I was startled from my thoughts by a loud and persistent ringing of the doorbell. As I approached the door, I could see through the glass the shape of a red car on the forecourt. I had a stab of irritation. It had to be Donna Kutash's Chevvy, and I thought I recognised her bulky shape, waiting. She was still leaning on the bell as I opened the door.

"In the shower, honey?" she asked.

I was going to have to be very pointed to get rid of Donna. She didn't receive messages delivered gently. She pushed past me, and walked into the house as though it was her own.

"Just calling to see if you're OK. We're here for the weekend. Where's Greg?"

"At home. Donna, I have to go down to the shops."

"Fine, honey, I'll take you. Two girls on a frolic. All the excitements of Clayburg."

"No, I need a little time."

She dropped her broad backside on a kitchen chair. "Time is something I have plenty of. Be my guest."

Donna was ten years older than me, a plump mother of three who always wore loose slacks and sweaters to cover her thick calves and bulging belly. Her hair was short, hennaed and curly. She had creamy unlined skin, and impertinent, rather protruding brown eyes.

"No thanks," I said, making it as final as possible.

At the same time that Donna was talking to me, she was checking, or rechecking since her last visit, whether the kitchen needed redecorating, whether my blender was as big as the one she kept at the lake, and how my cedar tiles were looking compared to her felt inlay.

Donna interrupted her assessment of the dècor with a softly spoken question which caught me unawares. "So who are you seeing?"

"What a crazy question."

"I hear an old boyfriend of yours is in town," Donna said, rolling her eyes suggestively.

"I don't have any old boyfriends or anybody but Greg!" I said, my voice rising sharply, and cracking slightly.

I had thought that in her earlier remarks Donna was merely probing around with her usual prurient curiosity, but this was what she really had in mind – Chadwin. People were talking. Chadwin had been talking. There could not be any other explanation. My spirits, which had been recovering, plunged down. What had Chadwin said?

"All right, dear. Take it easy. I didn't mean to step on your toes."

"I'm going into Clayburg for a hairdo," I said, trying to get back to a normal tone.

"I'll keep you company and read the mags," Donna said, as though it was ordained.

"No, Donna. I have things to do. It'll be a waste of time for you."

Donna was measuring the order of the room. "What are you doing, dear?"

"I'm cleaning up for the winter."

"Nice. I thought you might be preparing for a Forest Ranger on a rainy afternoon."

I ignored her. "Listen, Donna. I'm going on my own. Maybe I'll call in at your place on the way back, but there's a lot I have to do here."

"Nobody in Clayburg can do hair," Donna said flatly.

"It's a matter of saving time."

Donna smiled knowingly. "You don't have something going do you, Loren? I swear I won't tell."

"No."

I was as cold and forbidding as I could be.

"No?" Donna's eyes bulged with expectation. "Are you sure, darling?"

"Donna, who is saying things about me?"

Donna licked her lips and moved her shoulders, non-committal. "Nobody. It's kinda on the internet that you used to know Dwight Chadwin," she giggled.

I realised this was a crucial moment. Donna was like a bear scenting meat when it came to sexual gossip; she could smell it at a hundred yards. I put on a very faint, weary smile, and said, "That is really rubbish," moving my head slightly to dismiss baseless imaginings.

"Really?" Donna said, staring hard, trying to decide whether I was posing or not.

I could see she was preparing to wade more deeply into the subject with relish, and I looked at my wristwatch. "I'm afraid I'll have to get on with things now," I said curtly, turning my back on her and picking up my handbag.

"OK, dear. Bye,bye," she said, levering herself up from the chair.

She waddled out the front door, still grinning. But I heard the tyre-scream as she reversed her car irritably to turn it round.

I was twenty-three when I met Greg Stamford. My parents were dead. I thought I'd put the past behind me as far as anyone could.

I was reminded when I looked in the mirror, or when I saw what my sister Grace had become, a fragile shell of a woman; but I had learned to accept these things, and look forward.

In contrast to Grace, I was strong. I had struggled, part-time, to get a qualification in accountancy at Yonkers Polytechnic when I was a pool clerk in an insurance firm. I got a job as a junior in the accounts department of a firm in Trenton, NJ, taking Grace with me as a kind of companion and housekeeper. I had a natural facility with numbers, although the rest of my education had gaps. I had spent too much time as a kid over the kitchen sink, and cleaning house for my widower father, when I should have been at school. But I progressed fairly fast from my junior post, through the finance departments of three firms, before joining Ulex, first as an internal auditor, and then, when I was thirty-three, being promoted to financial controller.

Before I met Greg I had never dated a man, and had no thoughts of marriage. I lived a quiet life with Grace, and sometimes shared an apartment with co-workers and Grace. It wasn't that I was scared of men or disliked them. I had a full life with my job, a workout at the gym, various educational classes, and occasional weekends away with a trekking club. I met Greg on a trekking weekend in the Appalachians.

He was twenty-eight, quiet, unambitious, untidy in his dress, and rather conscious of his thin fair hair. He wasn't good-looking, but there was something refined and humorous about his face. He made me laugh a lot. I knew instinctively that he hadn't the self-confidence to make a pass at me. That made it easier for me to get to know him as a person whom I could trust completely.

One thing we had in common was this ability to handle numbers. We had fun with numbers games, but Greg was in a different league educationally. He was an economics graduate of New York State University. I found his middle-class background attractive and slightly unnerving. His father had been a dentist in Baltimore. Greg was used to a comfortable, genteel life-style which showed itself in a hundred small ways, from what he chose to eat or wear, to how he spoke. I was as blue-collar as he was white, although in my work career, this had been obscured. Greg never focussed on my class background or anybody else's for that matter. It wasn't an angle that interested him.

I loved Greg desperately when I got to know him. It didn't happen overnight. We were married quietly in Baltimore. I had no family apart from Grace, and few friends to invite to the wedding. Greg's mother, and his already married brother and sister, were glad to see him settle, although I wasn't quite the bride that they would have wished. But my looks, and the fact that I was no fool carried me a long way with them.

"He'll be easy for you to manage, that's for sure," Greg's sister said to me.

I had no thought of managing Greg, but by the time I was working at the Rochester head office of Ulex, I suppose I had quietly done a lot to change the tousled, slightly forgetful, maths wizard. Greg's bosses began to notice a smart, well-dressed man with a high-achieving wife, who was also an agreeable hostess. Greg was not ambitious himself, but he was clever, and his lack of egocentric drive made colleagues feel easy with him.

My advance in business may have been partly the result of a fear of insecurity. My father was unemployed for long periods. I couldn't go back to that. I had to advance. One part of me would have been happy to settle down as a wife and mother, but no children arrived. Both Greg and I were pronounced perfectly healthy by the doctors, and we waited for the lucky day. But with no children, I kept my career going. About seven years ago, a friend of Greg's sister, who played in the New York Philharmonic, had twin girls after an affair with another violinist. We were lucky enough to be in a position to adopt.

By the time we moved into our new house in Cedar Falls, I was completely fulfilled. Now, Chadwin's appearance seemed to threaten the calm, happy life I had created. I sat in the kitchen until it was dark, reasoning that it was absurd to feel threatened. What I really had to cope with was my unbridled imagination, and the nauseating feeling of knowing that the man was nearby.

After dark, I called Greg. I knew the children would be in bed. I couldn't face talking to them; they would know instantly of my turmoil from the tone of my voice, and I wouldn't be able to answer their innocent questions.

"Don't do too much, Loren," Greg said. "There's plenty of time before the cold spell."

"I can manage it."

Greg, sounding withdrawn, said he would call tomorrow. He, too, had picked up my mood.

"Being here is good therapy," I insisted.

"Donna Kutash called this morning. I told her you were up there. They'll be at their place this weekend. I asked her to look in, and buck you up a bit."

The Kutashs' cabin was a couple of miles around the shore.

"She's already been here. Honestly, Greg, Donna is a pain in the ass. I don't want her here, pushing me around, telling me what I need."

"Donna means well, Loren."

"The cow treats me as if I'm her office girl. If Marty wasn't your boss, I wouldn't give her the time of day!"

It was a tense conversation, and I was glad when it was over.

I stayed in the dark kitchen, bits and pieces of my life turning over in my mind inconclusively, like washing in a tumble-drier. Then I made up a bed in the spare room, slipped off my jeans, and crawled in without bothering to wash or clean my teeth. My brain was weary after flailing around with all the possibilities, and I slept.

At six am I was awakened by a thrush on the window-ledge. The heating was working, and the house was warm. I guessed that despite the sunlight outside, it would be chilly. I showered, put on another pair of jeans, a thick turtleneck sweater, and trainers. After a bite of toast from the loaf of bread I had brought with me, and a glass of orange juice, I went out for a walk.

I decided to take the main road rather than one of the forest tracks, which are soggy at this time of the year, and require boots. The road, as usual, was deserted. The pines stand up close to the edge; it's dark in there, whatever the time of day. At times I could hear an animal moving in the undergrowth, probably a deer. I walked in the middle of the road, away from the direction of the lake, the sun warming my face and shoulders. After half a mile or so, I came to a County utility truck, partially blocking the road, its hazard lights blinking.

A man in a khaki jacket was working in the ditch beside the road. He had a cage with an animal in it. I went over to him.

"What is it?" I asked.

He leaned back and looked up at me, holding the cage up so I could see.

"It's a rat, lady, a very big rat."

The bedraggled grey creature worked its nose and tail furiously behind the wire netting. I shivered. The badge on the lapel of the County man said, 'Pest Control Department, York County.' He explained that they mostly used poison, but trapped a few specimens to send to the laboratory for a disease analysis.

"You get used to them," he said, seeing my revulsion. "The drains round here are full of them."

"Is it an epidemic?"

"Hell, no, lady. It's good ole American families and the trash they drop in summer."

"Would there be rats in the drains below our place, 'Pine Hill', back there?"

"'Pine Hill'? That your place? I know it. Sure. All round there. No need to worry, lady. I'll be working past there."

I walked back to the lakeside. The wind was making white riffles on the water. I threw a few of the round gray stones into the tide. Some trees on the lake-edge were yellowing, but the pines formed a dominant green-black line around the shore. The chill wind drove me back to the house. The unpleasant thought of the rats stayed with me. I wondered how many were in the deep open channels that ran by the house, and whether they would come into the house.

During the rest of the morning I worked hard, cleaning, putting aside the linen and articles I would need to take back to Cedar Hills. I had just had a sandwich for lunch when the doorbell rang. I glimpsed again the lines of a scarlet car through the door-glass, as I went to answer. I knew the car, but the shadow in the doorway wasn't Donna.

Marty Kutash stood on the step, rocking slighly on the balls of his feet, perhaps to add something to the five feet five of him that wasn't already provided by his raised heels. Marty was a managing director, used to respect from a lot of employees. He was rippling his eyebrows, flashing his eyes over his big, splayed nose. I knew what he was about.

"Donna's not here, Marty," I said, blocking the entrance.

"Yeah, I know. I thought I'd come over, and you know, I mean, be neighbourly."

Marty's pink lips broke open to reveal two rows of dental crowns that looked like bathroom tiles. He made me uneasy. I had joked and chatted with him at parties, or when we went to his house for drinks or a game of cards, but I didn't like the thought of being alone with him. I could smell the rutting stag. I believed the Kutashs regarded Greg and me as prudes because we didn't respond to innuendos about swapping partners, or sleeping around. I found it difficult, but obviously necessary, to be genial with the Kutashs. But today I was too preoccupied to worry.

"How did you know I was here on my own?"

"Greg spoke to Donna on the phone," he said, raising his eyebrows hopefully.

"So where is Donna?" I asked, standing my ground.

"Aw, c'mon," he said, making a vague gesture with a square, beringed hand. "I don't bite."

The hell he didn't bite, I thought. I forced a lightness of tone. "Well, Marty, where is she?"

"Up at the cabin."

"She knows you're here?" I said, opening my eyes, and giving him a wise-ass look.

"Sure she knows," he said, crestfallen.

I thought that was a lie.

"I believe you know a friend of ours, Bucky Chadwin," he said, trying to swerve away from his own embarrassment.

"You introduced me at the club. Remember?"

"Naah. Not that. He knows you from way back," he added, with a nasty chuckle. "One of the good guys, huh?"

Chadwin had certainly been talking. The shit. And what could he conceivably say about the woman he had raped?

"I don't know what you're talking about," I said.

"Oh yeah, Loren."

"You're insulting me."

"Hey no. I didn't mean anything, Loren. Have it your way, baby."

I was both furious at Marty Kutash's impudent assumption that I had some kind of sexually interesting past, and wounded at the thought of the lies Chadwin must have told, or at least the grubby inuendos he must have implied. My temper and my hurt, both acidic, seemed to neutralise each other. I stood on the doorstep, impotent.

Just then over Marty's shoulder, crossing the road from the sewer to his truck, I saw the County officer. He had advanced to 'Pine Hill' as he had predicted. It gave me an idea. I didn't respond to Marty. I abandoned my defence of the doorway, and stepped past him on to the porch.

"Hey," I yelled to the man. "Any problem?"

The officer turned, waved his free hand, and held up a bunch of traps.

"Rats!" I said to Marty.

"Yeah," he replied, uninterested.

The rat-catcher moved a few paces nearer to the porch, perhaps thinking I wanted a report. I waited until he was close enough to hear me.

"Well goodbye, Marty," I said loudly. "I'm busy right now."

"Hey, Loren, wait a minute," Marty said, as I slipped past him, into the house and shut the door.

Marty was the type of man who would bang on the door to make a point, but he wasn't going to do that with the County officer watching. I went into the bedroom, where the rear windows overlooked the parking space. I could see the two men through the tinted windows without being seen. They chatted for a few moments, and then Marty shot a mean look at the house, and got back into his car. Chadwin had been talking to Marty, and Marty had been talking to Donna. And Chadwin wouldn't have been admitting a rape.

When it was dark, I heated up a TV dinner in the microwave. After a few unappetising fork-fulls I had another uncomfortable call from Greg.

"Grace must have overheard some of our call before. I think she wants to speak to you," he said.

I made it sound as though I was delighted. Grace was affected by all the emotional breezes which blew in the household. I had to try to put her at ease, although I doubted if I could.

I would have looked after my autistic sister whatever happened, but I held her close for another reason as well. I had always questioned whether in some way I was responsible for what happened to her that day in Yonkers. I was the older person, supposed to have some judgement. I was the one who suggested that we should walk through a deserted industrial area. I was the one who could and should have absolutely refused to get in the car. I was the one who didn't shout loud enough when we were in the car, and we didn't stop at the Dane supermarket. I was the one who misjudged the mood of the men, and failed to realise they would go as far as they did. Grace had no ability to assess. It was my call all along, and perhaps a more vigorous stand by me would have saved us both. This undermining thought was often behind my dealings with Grace.

So I said my pacifying words to her. I asked her about her art class. I concluded, "I'll see you tomorrow night, and I'm already feeling brighter for being up here in the quiet."

Later, I tried the television, but the bright lights and raucous voices on the screen – every channel – were incomprehensible. I showered and went to bed. My brain felt heavy, worked and worried to a standstill.

4

I packed the Jeep on Sunday morning and headed back to Cedar Falls. There was little traffic and the drive was another opportunity to try to get my thoughts in order.

Rochester, NY was a big enough city for me to avoid Chadwin indefinitely, but if we belonged to the same country club, and the same business community, and shared even a few acquaintances, he couldn't be avoided. I would always be on my guard, looking around crowded restaurants, wondering whether he was in the shopping mall. The chance of meeting him might not be all that great, but the possibility would always be on my mind. He would always be on my mind. Another worry was my sister. Grace lived on a fragile edge. Chadwin's presence in town meant that Grace too might have to confront the past, with serious consequences for her health. But that was probably rather remote.

A possibility was for us to leave Cedar Falls, get a transfer or new jobs, a long way away. My credentials, and Greg's, were good enough to do this, and we might even improve our prospects. But I was attached to our Park Drive home, the Cedar Falls area, and Chesterfield. The kids' school was good too. And my job. Greg was settled and advancing at Insel. Everything fitted neatly. It was part of me. It was me. Inside me, there was something which resisted the idea of running away, a thread of hot wire. *Why* should we run?

I still had a vivid memory of Chadwin's father at the court, a tall authoritative man with a purplish sheen on his cheeks, a dark astrakhan coat and steely hair, very much in charge of their party. He had put his benediction on the police, the prosecutor and the judge. He led the contemptuous sweep of the Chadwin party as they moved out of the court past me, in my neck-brace, my jaw still aching; they were heading to march right over my body in the corridor of the court unless I got out of the way. So I got out of the way, and tried to forget.

My life had been so tranquil in the last few years that Yonkers only came back in rare moments of weakness – until Greg's fateful mention of that name in the kitchen. My confused thoughts continued when I arrived home. I tried not to show a sign, but to be the serene, happy wife I usually was.

On Monday morning, Greg reminded me that on Wednesday, after work, we were having cocktails at the Garcias', and on Friday night I was supposed to be joining Kitty Calino's party for dinner and drinks at the club. The Friday date gave me an uneasy feeling. Abbott's Point had become Chadwin territory.

It was Greg's turn to take the twins to school, and I was in my office at eight-thirty sharp on Monday morning. I ran quickly through the schedule of work I kept on screen, and soon lost myself in a report on marketing costs. I was absorbed until it came to me that my company did business with Chadwin's. Not that this need ever lead to a link between us; they were both big companies; it was merely an unpleasant taint.

After work I called the secretary's office at the club, and asked one of the clerks to read me the list of latest members. Dwight Loughlin Chadwin II was on it; a family name as pretentious as his nickname was childish.

"The inaugural for those new members is on Friday, at six pm. Would you like to attend?" she asked.

I missed a heartbeat. As I had suspected, Chadwin was in the face of my date with Kitty Calino. Situations like this could arise again and again.

Abbott's Point was called a golf and country club. It had a golf course of national tournament standard, and regularly hosted matches of that calibre. It also had tennis and squash courts, pools and a gymnasium. A jogging track wound through the tens of acres of forest and around the lake. There was a café and two 'fine dining' restaurants. The membership committee, according to Greg, were open about race and religion, but there was an undoubted bias toward business executives and professionals from the upper ranks. The club was expensive, and it provided an exclusive venue for its hundreds of members which could be a focal point for family enjoyment, business and discreet politics at the same time. People who were members and lived in Cedar Falls would regularly find themselves either attending, or being invited to attend functions there. Chadwin's membership of Abbott's Point was therefore a serious worry to me.

I hadn't finally decided, but I was thinking of finding a reason to stay away from Abbott's Point on Friday. I found it impossible to make any clear plan to deal with Chadwin. I had to follow my instincts, and they were to stay as far away from him as possible. I was obviously perfectly well, but I could pretend I was ill on the night. I couldn't raise any objection to meeting Kitty. Her husband Dick was a colleague of Greg's at Insel. The Calinos had made us feel very welcome when we first moved to Rochester.

I turned the possibilities over, and decided to sound out whether Greg might call in at the club on Friday. I didn't want him at the club if I was going to be there on this occasion. On Thursday night I said, "Are you going to stop by Flinty's tomorrow?"

Joel Flint was an old buddy from Greg's New York State

days. It had become a practice for Greg and a few of Flinty's other cronies, to have a few beers, and a hand or two of poker, at the back of Flinty's bookshop in Chesterfield on a couple of Fridays a month.

"Yeah. I'm about due."

"I'll be with Kitty at the club."

"First guy back home opens the refrigerator!"

On Friday morning I was still indecisive about the date with Kitty. I swayed between apprehension and annoyance with myself. The annoyance barely resolved my decision. I was wearing a light grey suit for the office, but I selected a pair of tan slacks, a striped shirt, and some low-heeled buckskin moccasins from my wardrobe, and put them in a bag. After the crowd left the office – very promptly on a Friday – I could change in my room without interruption. That evening, as I looked at myself under the spotlights in the washroom, I had no reason to lack confidence, despite the damage Chadwin had done. My wheat-coloured hair framed my face. I didn't wear glasses or contact lenses. I had a healthy, sporty look, although I'm not an outdoor woman. The slight tan came from a bottle; too many of my golfing friends were beginning to look like dried walnuts. My figure had probably benefited from not having children; it was shapely in the waist yet rounded. I filled my clothes. I wasn't the bony racehorse type. I'm not overtly sexy. I never used my sexuality ever, except with Greg. But here I was, preoccupied with my looks as though I was going into a beauty contest. I asked myself if I was dressing up for Chadwin – that would have been incongruous and repellent; but I expect that there was an element in me that wanted to show that I wasn't a beaten-up Tarrytown broad any longer.

"Keep your head down, and see how it goes," I said to the mirror when I was ready.

"You can't go on like this," the mirror seemed to retort, but I ignored it.

I drove quietly on automatic pilot to the Abbott's Point parking lot, and sat in the Jeep watching the minutes flick by on the digital clock. At six-ten pm I locked the car and walked across the lot, up the steps, and into the lounge like a sleepwalker. The inaugural meeting was happening in one of the side-rooms. From the open doorway, I could see the golden back of Chadwin's head, and the dark bouffant hair of the woman with him.

At the bar I met Kitty and her friends, ordered a martini, and tried to lose myself in various conversations. After twenty minutes, I noticed the people from the new members' meeting drifting into the room. I was sitting on a high stool, watching the room in the mirror that backed the bar. I had an opportunity to see the woman I thought was Chadwin's wife, thin-lipped, sharp-featured, older than him, over forty. She had a sallow skin, and a lean figure. On her wedding finger, a thickness of rings glittered. Socialising carried Chadwin away from her, to the other side of the room. It wasn't difficult to keep my eye on that golden head.

While I carried on trivial talk with Kitty and my friends, the realisation had seeped through me that I didn't have the nerve, or the objectivity to face Chadwin. I had half thought that I wanted to test his attitude toward me. He had obviously recognised me, and said or implied to Marty that there was some previous connection between us. More than that, he must at least have hinted at a sexual connection. But what had he actually said? I wanted to try to reach some kind of understanding with him; we had to live in the same town. But I was breathless with nerves. My hands trembled. I had to lock my fingers around the stem of the glass. My expression, as I glimpsed it in the mirror, was a rictus.

I suddenly wanted to get out of the club, get home to Greg and the twins, and rethink all this. I made my excuses to Kitty, saying I was having a tough time at work. I slid off the stool, and pushed through the forest of bodies toward the door. In my distraction, I still had my martini glass in my hand.

"Oh, sorry!" a man's voice said, as he jolted my elbow, and splashed the few drops left in my glass on to the carpet.

Chadwin was turning, and rearing before me in the press of people. I ignored him and tried to press on.

"My fault," he said.

"It doesn't matter..."

I didn't look at the man. I could feel his eyes all over me.

"I'll get you another."

"I've finished. I'm going," I said, but he was blocking me.

"I insist."

"No," I said, for the first time meeting his casual stare.

He dropped his voice. "I was coming to see you..."

He moved before I could manage a dazed reply. He took my elbow, trying to steer me to the bar. I shook his fingers off instantly, but I yielded. *He had moved to intercept me*. Perhaps he, too, thought that we would meet eventually, and therefore the sooner the better.

Chadwin asked the barman for two martinis, and as the drinks were mixed, he maintained a loud monologue as though we were old acquaintances, about the club – how good it was, how much he disliked Rochester, and the problems of finding a suitable house. All this time, Chadwin was running his whitish eyes over me like a pair of hands, and keeping a lookout in the bar mirror for the approach of his wife. My voice had dried in a parched mouth.

"We have to meet again," he said, imperatively, his voice intimate under the babble of conversations around us.

"Never," I whispered.

"When are you usually here?" he asked as though I hadn't spoken.

I should have said, yes, it was reasonable that we meet, for the sole purpose of reaching an understanding that we would live as separately as we possibly could, but the man overawed me. I shook my head negatively.

Chadwin glanced hastily in the mirror and stiffened.

"Aren't you going to introduce me, Bucky?" Mrs Chadwin said, arriving in a cloud of gin and lime, and Christian Dior perfume.

Chadwin introduced me to Eve, and explained that he had accidentally spilled my drink.

"He's always doing that to young women," Eve Chadwin replied, languidly.

I participated dumbly in the exchange. Chadwin continued to ramble. There was an undertone. I understood Eve Chadwin's concerns only too well. After a few moments, Eve turned away brusquely to another group, irritated I suppose that her husband had cornered another female. I stepped away from Chadwin, intending to leave my drink, and walk out. I had hardly spoken a word. He clamped his hand on my arm again. His grip was firm – and I hoped invisible to the other people clustered around the bar.

"It's no use trying to avoid me. This is a goldfish bowl."

I jerked away, and pushed through the crowd to the door. The cold hit me at the entrance. I ran across the car park. When I slid behind the wheel I felt the strain of what had happened. I was weak. A meeting with Chadwin might be right; it was a mature approach. But I couldn't face him.

"I'll think about it," I said aloud to myself, as I started the engine.

5

The following Wednesday, I arranged for Rosanne to look after the twins as soon as Grace brought them home from school. I left work early, and drove aimlessly for a while, ending up at Monroe County airport. I parked, and sat in the coffee bar there, sipping an espresso and reading a magazine – actually just turning the pages, until six-thirty pm. I had to be in a neutral environment where time could tick away without affecting me, and I could think. The constant movement of the travellers left me in soothing isolation. I thought I had performed fairly well as a wife and mother and a financial executive since last Friday, but going to Abbott's Point again brought my worries to the surface.

I had a gym class at the club, and I was wondering whether I had the courage to attend. The chances of meeting Chadwin were remote, but the thought spoiled the place for me. Then I got annoyed with myself for being so weak. The club was part of my territory, and why should I withdraw because Chadwin wanted to speak to me? I pumped up my courage sufficiently. I drove to Abbott's Point.

I walked into the lounge, and my breath caught in my chest. I saw Chadwin immediately! He was seated with a group at the bar, back to the bar, with a clear view of the room. He was positioned to notice me come in, and he did. He stood immediately, and called my first name loudly as I walked, head down, toward the doors leading to the gym. His voice resounded across the nearly empty lounge. *He had been expecting me, waiting for me.*

I was all the more uneasy because one of the men with Chadwin was Marty Kutash. I had to turn around and acknowledge them. I stopped by the picture window looking out on to the eighteenth hole, shivering with repulsion. Chadwin had detached himself from his friends, and moved towards me.

"Hi, Loren, we've just had an afternoon's golf. It's a great course," Chadwin said with his kid's toothy smile. "How about a drink, or don't you touch liquor before you start pumping lead?"

"How do you know I have a gym class?"

"Whatsamatter honey?" Chadwin said, soothingly, as though he knew me intimately.

"Why are you following me?"

"We could go to another bar," he offered quickly, deaf to my words.

"Didn't you hear? I don't want even to see you in the distance," I said, trying to give the impression of composure.

"Like I said, we're in the same fishbowl."

"One of the people you're with works with my husband."

"Uh-huh, don't worry about Marty. I'll tell him I owe you an apology for last Friday."

I moved away, intending to abandon the workout class.

"I'll call you at your office," he said.

"No!"

"You'll regret it baby."

"What do you mean?"

He stroked his jaw with a hurt-child look. "I should call you on your private line. Let me know the number. It's less embarrassing than going through your PA. I believe you have a PA. And a staff. And a title. You're a smart girl. You've come a long way. Don't spoil it."

"I'm not going to talk to you," I said, choking on the monstrous implications of the vague threat.

"Oh, yes you will, honey."

Angry as I was, I could see there *was* a trace of sense in reaching an understanding with this misguided man. How else could I live from day to day? But at the moment, in the face of his presumption, my reason and my actions were out of sync. I broke away from him, and heard his laugh in my wake.

I gave Marty Kutash a friendly wave as I headed back toward the gym. It had taken only a few moments to talk to Chadwin, but I wondered at what cost. How would it appear to Kutash? As though I had called in, specifically to speak to Chadwin? I couldn't just leave the club. I went through the entrance to the gym, although I had no stomach for the workout. I hid in the washroom, and cried; they were tears of frustration.

I had another sleepless night. The thought of Chadwin's call, and when it would come, and what could be said, never left my mind. I had to force myself out of bed in the morning, drugged with tiredness.

At the office, I was on my third cup of coffee when Chadwin called. I let Sally put the line through, and then cut it before speaking. In a few moments, he was on the line again. This time I had to deal with him more frontally.

"Tell him I'm out," I said to Sally, trying to sound bored with a nuisance caller.

I didn't want to tell Sally not to put any future calls from Mr Chadwin through, because it was such a personal declaration that it would have created questions in her mind, although she didn't know who he was. Fortunately, Chadwin didn't call again. In the afternoon while I was working, whether I was talking to people, or on the computer, I railed in my mind at what an unfair world it was for women. We were supposed to be emancipated, and yet a macho male animal like Chadwin was pushing me around as he pleased, and I was retreating, retreating, trying to protect my reputation, myself, my life.

That night when Greg was asleep, I moved over tight on my side of our big sleigh bed, lying on my back, eyes open. I tried to see the situation as Chadwin might. He could be an unreasoning, swollen penis in human form, but that didn't square with his upbringing, college education and career. He had moved with success among sophisticated people, and he must have some insight into them. Surely a rational understanding between us was possible.

Meeting, just for an instant, after fifteen years, was one terrible stroke, but it was more than that. He now appeared to be talking about me to his new friends, *and* pursuing me. Actively pursuing. His overbearing tone didn't square with a man who simply wanted to reach an understanding with his former victim, and retire. I could be wrong about that. He was the bully-boy type. He probably tackled most of his relationships in football boots. Or, he could be so sexually jaded that the prospect of pursuing his victim after all this time had a special frisson, an excitement beyond his other encounters; a try-on which he would push for a distance, and then give up in the face of my resistance.

I didn't want to consider the one further possibility; that in a perverse way he wanted revenge. Revenge for being put in the dock to face criminal charges, for the embarrassment of his family; revenge for his own suffering while the outcome of the case was in doubt. Revenge for the pain he had unquestionably brought upon himself. I couldn't believe that he could really be that disordered.

If I was going to meet Chadwin, as he wished, be alone with him, there were two ways it could be: calm with an opportunity for serious talk, or angry. If it was going to be anger, I couldn't deal with a two hundred pounds plus man. He could beat me up, and walk away – unless I could restrain him. Restrain him? Yes, restrain him so that I could talk to him. If a woman wanted to restrain a monster like Chadwin, it could only be done with ropes, and a secret place to keep him.

My crazed mind wandered into this impossible territory, and led to a fantastic dream that night about the workshop at Chateaugay, which had some of the qualities of a safe and secret place. I could tie him up there and talk sense to him. I could force reason and decency down his throat with a lavatory brush.

In my dream, I was looking around the workshop with the idea of confining Chadwin there. It's deep under the house. You have to go through the garage at the front to get to it. If the garage doors were closed, as well as the workshop doors, nobody would hear anything out front, and the lakeside is entirely private. I looked at the walls of the workshop to find a pipe, or a bracket which he could be tied to, but there was nothing. All I could do, I reckoned, would be to secure Chadwin on a frame on the floor, so that he was spread-eagled, flat on his back. He wouldn't be in any pain. He'd be able to listen and talk. In my dream, I bought a double mattress, and ropes in Clayburg. I invited Chadwin to the house. I hit him over the head with a baseball bat. I dragged his body down the stairs to the workshop, and tied him to the mattress. When he became conscious, he only swore at me. He wouldn't acknowledge the horror of what he had done to me. My plan had failed. In frustration, I tied a rat-trap around his groin, with the open end over his penis. Inside the cage was a hungry, scurvy rat.

I woke up suddenly, sweating at having created a medieval inquisition in my imaginings, but more than that, deeply depressed at not being able to get any acknowledgment from Chadwin about the hurt he had inflicted.

Greg found me sipping a glass of milk, sitting on the end of the bed in the dark, at three in the morning. He flicked the bed-lamp on.

"What's the matter?"

I should have told Greg then, let the whole ugly story come out – but I felt as though I would be fouling the warm security of our bedroom.

"Oh… those work problems."

"It's not like you. You're always saying to me, if you can't cut it, it's no use busting yourself trying. Maybe you should be thinking of making a move."

"I'm thinking about it."

When I lay down beside my husband, and felt him cuddle in around me, I had decided to go with my first thoughts about Chadwin – that he was taking a bull-headed approach to an understanding between us, or at most, that he was a bored voluptuary seeking a thrill, but in the end, amenable to reason. I therefore had to let Chadwin know clearly and calmly how I felt, and that could only be done by talking with him, preferably face to face.

I accepted the phone call at my office the next day with a grim heart.

Chadwin spoke with a voice of oily expectation, and sighed theatrically when I agreed to meet.

"I knew you'd see reason, Loren."

"The only reason I'm seeing you is that we need to agree that we will never ever, ever, ever have anything to do with each other."

"That's kind of difficult in this one man and a dog dump, but we can talk about it."

We haggled about a date, and I insisted on the club as a place, around 6pm the forthcoming Friday. It was public, and we both had a reason to be there. At least it was better than my office, a bar, a park or the telephone. I wanted to get Chadwin off my mind as soon as possible.

On Friday when I arrived at Abbott's Point I saw that Mr and Mrs Chadwin were playing in the mixed foursomes. I hadn't reckoned on Mrs Chadwin being around. In my view this put an end to the possibility of having a private talk with her husband. When I was in the ladies'washroom, Eve Chadwin came in. She might have seen me, and followed me in, because I suspected that in the few moments when we were introduced, she may have divined that my connection with her husband was not about an accident with a glass. She remembered me. Recognising somebody in the mirror is somehow less personal than turning toward them. I had tied my hair back in a ponytail, and I was wearing a black trouser suit from Saks.

"You look stunning, my dear," Eve said.

"It was a present."

Eve raised her eyebrows which were plucked to a thin line. "A generous and tasteful husband – how rare!"

"No, a sister-in-law who thinks I need a bit of style."

"How candid of you."

As we were putting the final touches to ourselves, I had the feeling Eve wanted to speak. She arrested me a few steps from the washroom door, and paused to clip her Gucci handbag. I felt no animosity.

"And do you think *my* husband has the rare qualities I mentioned?"

"How could I possibly have the slightest idea?"

Eve's question interested me less than a grain of salt, but it showed that she understood, with the uncanny antennae of a wife.

"I thought you knew him!" Eve cackled, exhaling sharply and distending her nostrils.

"You're mistaken," I said, and to exclude any further enquiry, I asked how they were settling down.

As Eve began to speak, it came to me with complete clarity, that there might be a way of dealing with Chadwin which I had not thought of before: tell his wife. Tell her the facts without any embellishment. It would be an explosive revelation, but it would bring to a halt any plans Chadwin might have to harass me. I knew very little about Eve. She was a successful investor, and it was gossip that she had rescued Chadwin from a deal which had gone sour, and threatened him with bankruptcy. She would undoubtedly be a strong influence over him. But it would be unwise to embark on this course without telling Greg first. He might be drawn into it. I needed to think about the implications of telling Eve more carefully, and that included telling Greg my story, to start. As we walked toward the lounge, I contented myself with my denial.

Eve said that Rochester was an awful place. It had been raining and windy ever since they had arrived, and there were no decent shops. Chesterfield was no more than a kind of doll's village. Cedar Falls was pretentious and indescribably boring. The only way they would be able to endure it was by flying regularly to their place in Florida. Eve mentioned she had two children from a previous marriage who also hated the move. She admitted that they were spoilt and demanding.

"I sometimes think children delight in torturing their parents," she said.

Eve was a brittle woman with a variety of postures and poses. Elegant, attractive and rich as she was, lines of anxiety were beginning to be chiselled around her mouth. Her skin was drying and shrinking. And she was Chadwin's wife.

Chadwin ensured that we appeared to drift together in the crowded room. I saw him, after a while, discreetly near me at the end of the bar. His glance wasn't lecherous; it was chilly and knowing. He moved to a place beside me when he could, and began to talk. His first marriage was written off as a stupid mistake. By the sound of the vacations he and his wife were having in Europe, they had a lot of money. I looked around to see who was watching us, and decided probably nobody. This was a neutral place to be seen with Chadwin. He was bending over me proprietorially from his six feet. The way he moved his head and shoulders exuded a virility that would have made me laugh, if he had been any other man. He was wearing a plain grey suit cut closely to his figure, and a button-down shirt open at the throat. The clothes were a platform for his red-gold hair. Women gave him a second look and he knew it. He could see I was jumpy and inattentive.

"Come out to the car, and we can talk."

"What about your wife?"

"Eve's gone to a book-signing in Chesterfield."

"You don't do them."

"I don't read fiction, baby. I prefer real life," he guffawed.

I knew how risky Chadwin's proposal was. I didn't trust the man, and I didn't want to be seen consorting with him. But I couldn't go on with phone calls and suggestive meetings in a crowd. Chadwin already had the wrong idea about me. The very knowingness of his attitude demanded an understanding, so in spite of my misgivings, I decided to go.

Chadwin eased away, and headed for the door. I waited a few moments and followed. When I got to the front steps, I could see Chadwin in the half-dark, headed for the far side of the parking lot where there were few cars. Perhaps he had parked with the idea that he might lure me there. No. I was an adult going to have a necessary talk with another adult. Chadwin pointed to his car when I approached, and I was relieved to see it was quite small. I walked around the rear where the badge said XJ12S, a sports convertible, very low to the ground, with two aircraft type seats in front, and lots of controls between them. The car park was floodlit, and there was still light in the sky. I would have suggested we talk outside, but for the gritty gusts of wind which swept across the lot.

I think Chadwin would have liked to grab me when he got inside, but he slid back behind the wheel, defeated by his surroundings.

"Bloody car! It's only good for driving."

I launched myself like a suicide off a bridge. "You obviously recognised me when you first saw me."

"Of course," he said, smugly. "I've often wondered what happened to you. I thought you might have made a living as a call girl."

I restrained myself from leaving the car. "You want to be insulting, like you were the person who got hurt."

In the half-light, his face looked metallic, different surfaces reflecting like plates of copper, yet quite open and honest-looking.

"You caused me a wagon-load of grief, Loren, but that was long ago."

"Big deal. *You* had grief. Why are you after me?" I said, my breast heaving, trying to control the turbulence.

"Why not? We're both looking for fun."

His hand groped ineffectively across the drive housing, fumbling my knee.

"Get away! I'm Loren Reynaud. The People versus Chadwin and Schultz!"

Chadwin's arm slid away, and he was stilled. A mistiness clouded his features, a heave of air into his barrel chest.

"You were just a little bag of trash – then, but you've put on some polish since."

I heard the label which had been assigned to me implicitly in the Westchester County court. The insult generated a white heat under my skin, but I took it.

"You didn't expect to meet me at your country club. I have a respectable life here."

"Do you?" Chadwin said, flexing his jaw disdainfully.

"I don't want my life spoiled by harassment from the man who raped me!"

"Goddam it, Loren, I have forgotten all that stuff that happened centuries ago."

But I knew he hadn't forgotten, and the past had been reawakened for me, too. A wound of yesterday, still bruised and bleeding.

"Can you understand how nauseating it is to see you, let alone speak to you?"

"Why are you here, then?"

"You dick! I'm here because you threatened me. I'm here because of what happened in Yonkers, and nearly drove my sister crazy. I don't know you. I only know a brute from the past who is threatening me now."

I was beginning to doubt whether the spoiled, over-privileged savage at the Westchester court had become, or would at least behave like a sensible career executive with a family and a reputation to sustain.

"So why have you given me the come on?" Chadwin persisted, amused now.

"How can you say that, you fool? There must be something wrong inside your head. I'm prepared to talk to you. I want us to work out how we're going to handle this. How we can both have a life here."

"Talk? Shit. Let's have a screw. It's what we both want."

"Never!"

"Listen, Loren. I'd go easy on this. My advice to you. You

have a nice job, and your husband is well placed. Once people know about you. You know? People can't handle this."

"Know about me! I haven't done anything wrong. You're the one who's done wrong."

"People won't see it that way."

My face was streaming wet, tears of impotence and fury.

"Listen man. You were sentenced for assault on me. Don't try to tell it any other way!"

"I don't have any convictions, baby. My record is clean."

I could take no more. I heaved the heavy door open, and ran across the lot to the clubhouse.

6

I went into the washroom, cleaned up my face and set my clothes straight. On the drive home my tear-swollen eyes, and unsteady hands, set the Jeep shuddering and sliding on the blacktop. Greg's car was in the drive when I arrived. He had apparently come straight from the office instead of going to Flinty's. He noticed my clothes, and my agitation, and came up to me and put his arms around me.

"Hey, who's a knockout?"

"I've just been to the club."

"Fine, sugar. Fine. You look good. That's the outfit Penny sent you, right? The one you said you never go anywhere smart enough to wear."

"Compete with Kitty or die."

"What's the trouble?" he asked, holding me at arm's length.

He took my chin and forced me to look at him.

"Is there somebody else?"

He fired the words like a rifle shot, flinching as he pulled the trigger. My behaviour had created this doubt. In trying to excuse my worries with overwork, I hadn't thought sufficiently about the impression I was really creating.

"God, no! I love you Greg and I've never loved anybody else!" I said, burying my face in his shoulder.

Greg released himself, went into the lounge, and poured himself a shot of bourbon from the liquor cabinet, a sure sign that he was disturbed. He came back to the doorway, leaning on the frame, sipping the drink.

"You're a very attractive woman, Loren. Men are always looking at you. I notice it."

I felt drained of energy. I couldn't embark on the monstrosity of the Chadwin story.

"I just feel a bit rough at the moment, Greg. Could you fix me a drink as well?"

What did Chadwin mean when he said, *Once people know about you*? As though I had a past to be ashamed of!

I had a restless night, thinking about packing up the family and running, but in the headachey sourness of dawn, I decided I was going to take control. The stolen minutes at Abbott's Point had been useless. I had utterly failed to get my point across.

On Monday morning, I phoned Chadwin from my office, my gut wrenching. He came on the line with a smarmy tone.

I said flatly, "Look, I don't want to leave it the way we did at the club."

Chadwin's lascivious laughter jarred me. "Neither do I honey, neither do I!"

"We need to understand each other if we're going to live in the same environment," I said slowly, almost spelling it out.

"Yes, of course we do," Chadwin replied, with mock-seriousness.

"Well, the understanding has to be this – I'll lay it out for you: I don't want to ever have anything to do with you. Do you get that? Do you understand?"

"I hear you," he said with a fake yawn.

"I'll keep clear of you and your friends, and I want you to do the same."

"Not possible. For example, Marty Kutash."

"I can gladly keep away from him, and I will."

"It won't work, Loren."

"If you come near me again, I'll call the police and have you charged with harassment. I swear I will!"

"You'll land yourself in a heap of trouble if you do that. Yes, mam. You could get your reputation in this town kinda sullied."

"I swear to God I'll have you charged!"

I cut off the call. I had delivered my message in a low, I suppose tremulous voice, which concealed my temper. Afterwards, I mouthed curses on Chadwin silently, my head in my hands. And there was a streak of anxiety too. What *could* Chadwin do?

Then I noticed that Sally was standing by the open door. She was free to come in when she liked, and might even have heard part of the conversation.

"Can I help, Loren?"

"Must have been a bug in my breakfast fruit. Could you get me a tablet, Sally?"

I remained at my desk, and went over the encounter again. I had hoped, simplistically, that with one virulent dose of telling, I could relegate Chadwin to the back of my mind. I had hoped that he could fade into a figure in the crowd, a name amongst many in a conversation. I could not be sure I had succeeded. I had to hope that Chadwin's cruel desire to intimidate somebody whom he mistakenly took to be in his power, would now fade. I couldn't have made myself plainer. And there was nothing in what I had said, *nothing,* which could conceivably be interpreted as giving Chadwin any encouragement. I hoped fervently that I might never hear from him again.

In the next few days, I began to look on the optimistic side. I might, despite Chadwin's posturings, have won. Perhaps there *was* a future for the Stamford family in Cedar Falls. But I was too dispirited to go to Baltimore with Greg and the children on their annual visit to see his parents. I felt the need to be alone, and I told Greg that I would stay at home.

I thought I might go up to the lake at the weekend, after Greg had gone. I longed for peace away from work, away from the children, and even Greg. Grace would be busy with her own interests in Chesterfield over the weekend, so 'Pine Hill' would be mine. I made a messy explanation to Greg of my reasons, aware at the same time that I was chipping away at our warm relationship. I came out with a touch of finishing the mothballing, and wanting to think work problems through. He looked at me searchingly.

"And you're going up to the lake this weekend as well."

He was suggesting that my explanation wasn't good enough; that I had an ulterior motive.

Greg usually took a week of his leave every year with his mother. At first, we all used to visit, but I didn't get along with Mrs Stamford senior, and stopped going regularly. She was what neighbours call a dear old lady, charming and patient. But she was tolerated rather than loved by her own blood. She found flaws in everybody, and mine were irreparable. Despite my devotion to Greg, my performance as a mother, my intelligence, my good appearance and my career, I was always, to her, the daughter of an unemployed auto-worker from Tarrytown. In my present low state I couldn't subject myself to Mrs Stamford.

Greg knew my reservations about staying with his mother very well, and a small excuse to go to Chateaugay on my own would have sufficed. I over-egged it by going on about refuse attracting rats, and the rotten bananas I had found in the folds of one of the tents. I'm not a great house-keeper, so this didn't sound quite like me. What Greg might have been thinking – and I couldn't blame him – was that I had an assignation with a man at the lake. Because this simply wasn't true, I may have given it too little weight.

I had slept badly over the weekend. I couldn't entirely rest with the idea that I had dealt with Chadwin. My mind was grasping at the problem as in a dream, where your most reasonable positions are rejected, or not understood by others, and you can't understand why. Greg had tuned into my mood, and was trying to be his old impeturbable self, but at bottom, he was jealous. The only way to reassure him, was to tell the whole story. But I had a subconscious fear that he might react like my father, and regard me as in some way blemished. It was a thought I tried to dismiss, because Greg was a generous spirited man. I was also tormented by regret that I hadn't told him years ago. Having to tell him now suggested I hadn't trusted him earlier.

Then, I argued to myself, but for the remote chance that Chadwin's path would cross mine in future, I could have got away with silence. It had been my problem alone before Chadwin came to town, and I had buried it. But now the past had resurrected itself in a grotesque way.

On Wednesday, Greg and I took the girls into Chesterfield for a treat at McDonald's. Greg was perfunctory in his manner towards me. Tonight would have to be the night to tell him, unless I wanted to protract an estrangement. Later, when the children were in bed, and Greg had mixed himself a drink, and sat in the lounge without a book, the CD player and television pointedly not switched on, the moment had come. His silent attitude was that something was due from me. I sat down in one of the armchairs facing the couch, and refused a drink.

"I'm absolutely not having an affair, Greg. There's no man in my love life but you, and there never has been."

"Thanks. That's a relief. I know you said so before, but..."

He seemed to melt. He ought to have known that I meant it. "What is it, then?" he asked sympathetically. "I mean, work ... You've always been on top of that. You're a fighter. Some kind of personality clash?"

"I told you, it's work."

I was clinging to the half-hope that I had dealt with Chadwin, that he would be a figure in the distance if he materialised at all. I made up a story about back-biting at the office. I named people whom Greg had met. It was weak. It was a lie. I could see Greg wanted to believe me, but wasn't convinced. His manner with me was distant for the rest of the week. He entirely ceased making his usual mild jokes about everything around him, and he didn't cuddle up in bed.

On Saturday I stuck to my resolution to go to the lake on my own. When I reached 'Pine Hill' I was still determined to try to get through on my own. I had heard nothing more from Chadwin, and my clear determination may have stilled him, despite his bluster. I resumed my clean-up, and by mid afternoon I was feeling tired, and thinking of relaxing in the sun on the patio with a cup of coffee. I heard a car on the forecourt. I opened the door. It was Greg.

He looked at me shyly. He was uncertain. I didn't have to ask why he was there, and he didn't have to tell me. I went down the steps to the car, and put my arms around him. I stopped myself saying, 'There's nobody here, and there won't be. I'm quite alone,' or anything crass like that. He loved me and I was treating him badly. In my preoccupation with Chadwin, I hadn't realised how badly. He had just driven a hundred miles with a knife in his heart. I took his hand and led him upstairs. I shut and locked the front door, and drew him into the bedroom. I pulled off my sweater and slipped out of my jeans.

"Come on, my love," I said, and he began to undress.

We made passionate love, and when we were propped up in bed afterwards, with a highball each, I said, "It's not work, Greg. It's something I don't know how to deal with..."

Greg was feeling good. He was smiling. "If it's not me, and it's not work – that's good … great… " Then he sat up straight, serious. "My God, it's not your health, Loren, is it?"

"This is something else, something completely else…"

"Well if it isn't your health, that's good too …"

"You know I told you about Grace, what happened to her?"

"Grace? You mean years ago? Being attacked?"

"What I didn't tell you was that I was attacked too."

Greg's brow creased, and the light in his eyes intensified as he recalled what I had told him. Perhaps his recollection of my skimpy outline of the facts was as lurid as the reality.

"Oh, God, you poor thing… but why now? I want to hear about this, Loren – if you want to tell me."

"I didn't tell you before, because I thought I could bury it forever."

"I think I understand. Just talk. Get it off your mind. What happened?" Greg said, gently.

"I was raped. I was nineteen."

The words, as softly as I spoke them, couldn't be denied their harsh meaning, and hung in the space before us in the bedroom, an ugly cloud. Greg absorbed the reality behind the words. He winced. A net of lines appeared on his face. He looked away.

"It's a long time ago," he began in a thick voice. "And there's no particular reason why it should worry you now. We have a wonderful life together… Would you like to see a counsellor?"

"What happened in the past is dictating the present."

"How do you mean?" he frowned.

"Because the man is in town."

"Jesus! You've seen him?"

"Met him."

Greg's jaw clenched, and he paled. "Have I met him?"

I nodded. "Chadwin. Dwight Chadwin."

Greg's mouth opened slackly, gobbling. "The Hudson man? The man – his wife – I wanted you to meet?"

"I couldn't be sure it was him until I saw him at the club."

While Greg shrank in the bed, I tried to begin the story. But Greg wasn't capable of listening. He was shattered.

"Where does it stand now?" he asked after a minute.

"I don't know. I may be wrong… I feel he wants to hurt me."

"The scumbag. I'll have to see him."

"What would you say?"

"I don't know… Tell him to keep clear."

I felt a surge of affection for Greg, but he looked frail, and hunched, his fingers twiddling with the empty glass. I compared the brash, ox-like Chadwin with his golden head.

"No. Whatever we do, let's do it together," I insisted.

I asked Greg if he had organised Grace and the twins for the weekend, and he had. I think he had no idea how the weekend would develop when he left Park Drive.

"Let's stay until tomorrow, and do a few things around here," I said.

We worked together, packing up the house and workshop for the winter. We clung together like children that night.

Greg was quiet about what I had told him on the drive back to Cedar Falls, and when we arrived home on Sunday afternoon the time was full of the children. On Monday morning, when I went down to breakfast, Grace had made Greg's coffee and toast; he was sitting by the window, ignoring it, looking out absently at the children playing on the lawn which was white with dew.

"Greg, they're in their school clothes, and the lawn is soaking!"

Greg was turned away from me, looking but not seeing. "Do you think we should make plans to go away?"

"I've certainly thought of it."

"I mean, you can't avoid this man. It isn't just Abbott's Point. It's the business community, the street. It's mutual acquaintances."

He hadn't noticed that Grace had come into the room. And she must have heard this and seen our dour expressions.

"Can you get the girls in, Grace?" I asked. "See whether their socks and shoes are dry."

When she had gone, I said, "I know, I know, Greg, but something sticks in my gut about running away. I haven't done anything wrong."

"Sure, it sticks in my gut too, but in the longer term, Loren, could you tolerate this person *anywhere* near you?"

"I thought I could if we could each agree to look the other way. Now I'm not sure."

"Bloody swine! Do you know I was thinking of inviting the Chadwins to our Thanksgiving party. He's a big pal of Marty's!"

That night when we were in bed, I discussed with Greg my idea that one way to stop Chadwin would be to talk to his wife.

"Maybe we could get a better understanding that way," I said. "If she knew he had come on to me, especially with the past, I think she'd say enough to him to cool him off."

"That would shock her, and maybe cause damage to their marriage," Greg said.

"It would."

Greg thought about this. "I feel sorry for her...but Chadwin is some kind of sadist who is seeking to screw up our lives. So yes, it could be the right thing. What Chadwin said to you in his car at the club is something completely beyond civilised behaviour."

"OK. I'll see her. In a strange way, it'll almost be a relief to tell her."

"I reckon I ought to be there. Mrs Chadwin should know that you and I are completely solid on this, Loren."

"I think woman to woman is better. If you were there... No. It's between Eve Chadwin and me."

Grateful as I was for Greg's support, I felt that in some way that I couldn't define, it wouldn't be right for him to be there. He would be an awkward presence.

"I don't know. But if you say so..." he said.

I made discreet enquiries from one of the girls in the office at Abbott's Point, and found that Eve Chadwin played golf on Wednesday afternoons with a women's group. I resolved to go to the club, find her, and ask if I could speak to her privately for a few minutes.

I located Eve Chadwin in the bar on the following Wednesday, and in moments we had found seats in one of the smaller, vacant committee rooms. Eve did not hesitate in the slightest when I said I would like to talk to her privately.

"Now, Loren Stamford, what is troubling you," Eve said, settling herself in her chair.

She spoke as though she was chairing a meeting, and her eyes were keen. I had planned how I might begin, but lost the thread.

"You remember my name," I said.

"I was introduced to you by my husband, was I not? And we spoke, here, one day. My husband explained that he knew you many years ago. Although you denied it when we spoke."

"He raped me fifteen years ago, and a friend of his raped my sister."

Eve looked up at the ceiling, tightened her mouth, and with the smallest smile said, "A lot of girls say that."

"It's true, there was a court case..."

"Save the gory details, my dear. I already know them. Now, how can I help?"

"You don't know. You only know what that animal told you!"

"Please be calm, Loren – if I may call you that. What do you want to see me for?"

"Your husband is harassing me. He's ringing me up at the office. He's threatening me."

"What is he threatening?" Eve Chadwin asked, like the chair of a meeting elucidating rather boring facts.

"He's going to ruin my reputation, and my job, if I don't go to bed with him!"

"I think that's a bit fanciful, my dear. I mean, how could he ruin your reputation if you refuse?"

"By misrepresenting what happened in the past. Talking to people."

"Well, if you have something to hide…"

"I don't!"

I had lost my way with Eve Chadwin. She was stony, and completely unmoved. I'm not a mousy person. I can debate quite well. But on this subject, I was a puddle of mud. However, my wrath was rising, as much at my own ineptness as at Eve Chadwin.

"Look, Mrs Chadwin, get your ape of a husband to stop phoning me. I'll never, never have sex with him, and if he approaches me one more time, I'll complain to the police!"

Eve Chadwin fingered her gold makeup compact contemplatively. She had removed it from her hand-bag as a signal that she was waiting to freshen up, and move on. "Are you sure you haven't been bothering him?"

"After what I've said to you!"

Eve shrugged carelessly. "That's what he says."

"He's a filthy liar!"

"There are always two sides, Loren, my dear – sometimes more!"

Eve Chadwin, brassily bright, was sitting straight-backed in her chair, watching me sharply. I had made not the slightest impact. I felt the tears coming, and I rushed out of the room.

I told Greg when I got home.

He considered glumly for a moment. "She's just playing for position," he said. "She's not going to admit her husband is a shit in front of a stranger. You put the message across, Loren, and Chadwin will certainly get the acid from his wife."

He made me feel I'd done something useful. Then he broke into a big grin.

"I've got something to tell you. I've been in touch with an executive search agency. There's a top corporate planning job going in Buffalo, in an electronics company about the same size as Insel. I had a look at them on the internet. Could be right for me. I need to find out more, but if I could get it, it would be a step up."

I was astonished by his decision, and the speed of his move – not like him at all.

"Are you sure you want to do this?" I asked.

We talked for a while, and eventually agreed that he should apply if the job seemed appropriate. It would do no harm. It didn't necessarily mean we were committed to leave Cedar Falls. We hadn't actually said it aloud, but both of us were inclined to run. What was most important to me was to try to recover the peace of mind we had before Chadwin appeared in Cedar Falls. Alongside that contentment, the idea of courageously facing Chadwin down seemed unimportant. We weren't fighters for truth.

In normal circumstances, if Greg and I were changing jobs,

mine would be the first consideration, but I hadn't the spirit, or the will, to face job interviews. We decided I would take my chances of landing work, if and when Greg had a new post.

The proposal to move from Cedar Falls, which became more explicit between us day by day, freed me in a sense. Greg said we had to accept it like the wind and the rain, and stop asking why. Our home could have burned down, Insel or Ulex could have gone bust. Lots of uncontrollable forces could have moved us out of the district. Unfortunately, the arrival of Chadwin was one of them.

With this tentative decision to run, I found it easier to go to the office. I stopped worrying so much about whether any dirty gossip which had passed between Chadwin and Marty Kutash had seeped out to a wider audience. In a few months I could be out of this job, and out of this town.

On Saturday morning Grace went to her art class, and I did some shopping in Chesterfield. It was unseasonably warm enough for Greg and I to have a leisurely coffee and croissants in the garden at eleven. We sat under the sun shades, and started to talk about the move to Buffalo; it was disturbing to be enjoying the garden, and thinking of leaving it.

Greg said that the Buffalo job might fall through, but our intention to leave wouldn't. The head-hunters had told him that there were a number of corporate planning vacancies in the state at the moment. Greg wanted to try to sell the Chateaugay place now, before the winter. Otherwise it would have to wait until spring, and we might not be here to deal with it. There was usually a steady demand for the limited number of places on the lake, and I agreed. We anticipated that Park Drive would also sell quickly.

It eased the aggravation to make a practical move toward leaving. We decided I would go to the lake when Greg was in Baltimore, inventory the contents of the house, and instruct agents in Clayburg and Rochester to put it on the market. Later we would have to arrange transport for the things we wanted to keep, probably the sailboats, and our outboard speedboat.

Greg was unexpectedly late home from the office the next night, and when he came in his skin was grey, and he was without the slightest touch of humour as he embraced me.

"What's the matter?"

The children were upstairs with Grace, and he sagged down on a chair in the kitchen.

"I've seen Chadwin."

"I thought you weren't going to do that…I mean, our plans to move…"

I couldn't help showing that I questioned this.

"I *had* to do it Loren…"

But I did have a feeling of relief. I hadn't wanted to drag Greg into the mess actively, but the idea that I had my husband out there, supporting me, was very comforting. Greg seems to be an easy-going person, but there are times when he can insist on a point, no matter what.

"You didn't tell me, Greg."

"It wasn't a matter for agreement between us. You'd only say what you've already said. That I should leave it to you. But seeing the Chadwins was what I had to do, and I did it. It's a gut thing, Loren. I have to hold my head up."

"What happened?"

"I snagged Chadwin when he was over at Insel, visiting Marty, being shown the works. I had been thinking how I was going to see him. You know … it's a difficult thing to discuss anywhere. Anyway, there he was. I took him aside. Marty and others may have noticed. I didn't give a damn. We talked outside the john. The only place I could find. I said, "Stop bothering my wife. Stay away from her. If you don't I'll get the police involved. What do you think he said?"

"I'll guess he blamed me in some way, twisted the facts."

"You're right. He laughed and said, 'Get her to stop bothering me.' He said you were chasing after him, phoning him, asking for meetings. He treated it all as a joke."

"I did phone him to make a meeting."

"Everything you do will be construed against you, Loren."

"Do you wish you hadn't talked to Chadwin, Greg?"

"No. I had to do it, whatever the outcome. He's a smooth-tongued liar. I ended up saying, 'I've spoken to you now, and if I find you're getting in touch with my wife again, there'll be trouble.' Chadwin just sneered, and said I should take my wife in hand."

"So it's done no good," I said disconsolately.

"Yes, I think it's done *some* good. However arrogant and confident Chadwin is, it's a warning."

It may have been wishful thinking, but I believed Greg was right. Then Greg surprised me again.

"And I've spoken to Mrs Chadwin. I got her phone number from the club on a pretext about a game, called her, and went to their home by invitation this afternoon."

I was astounded. "What good could that do after she had rubbished me…?"

"It's a matter of piling on the pressure, Loren. We've both complained to these people now, and I think that's better than having kept quiet, whatever line they take. Chadwin will get an additional needle from his wife as a result of my visit, and whatever she says to us, she's going to be suspicious that there's something in what we say."

"What did she say?"

"Oh very civilised, offered me coffee, and pooh-poohed it as silly talk, suggesting as she did with you, that her husband had complained too, and maybe you were over-sensitive or had something to hide."

"I sure have got something to hide; a dead rat in the closet."

We agreed that in both facing the Chadwins, we had made some small positive steps toward putting up a bulwark against Dwight Chadwin, and that we had to do this, whether we were leaving town or not.

Greg and the twins had left for an early plane to Baltimore. I sat for a while in the lounge with the windows open, a chill breeze coming in from the garden. At this time on a Saturday, the neighbourhood around the house, so quiet during the week, came alive with the sound of children, lawnmowers, dogs, radios and neighbours doing odd jobs and yarning on the lawns.

I dressed in a sweater, an old grey roll-neck, and a pair of jeans whitened at the seams with washing. I tied my hair in a pony tail. No makeup. No perfume. I ate a little muesli with strawberry yoghurt for breakfast, and left a note for Carrie about the cleaning, and an envelope with Carrie's pay on the kitchen bench. I was ready well before I needed to leave. I could hear Grace moving around upstairs. I wandered through the comfortable, well-used downstairs rooms of the house, thinking how happy we had been here.

My sister was getting ready for her art class. I called goodbye. Grace came quickly downstairs looking pale.

"Tell me what's happening, please Loren."

It wasn't any use trying to fob her off. Grace had overheard snippets of talk between Greg and me over past weeks. She knew something serious was troubling us, and she probably connected it with the past.

"We're going to sell 'Pine Hill' and this house, and we're going to move to Buffalo. There's nothing to worry about."

"It's those awful men, isn't it?"

I hesitated.

"They're here... and they're going to do it again."

"No, never. You're perfectly safe, Grace."

"But they are here."

"One of them is."

"Which one?"

I told her about seeing Chadwin at Abbott's Point. I said it didn't mean anything, but in any event, Greg and I had worked out a way of dealing with the situation, and we would all come through without any trouble. But I left a very morbid sister.

I went outside and I was about to climb into the Jeep when I thought that I should make arrangements for Grace to have some company over the weekend. I knew that the Fredericksen's next door would be pleased to invite Grace for supper. I went back inside and found Grace. I asked her if she would like to go to the Fredericksen's.

"I'm going to a film with friends from my class this afternoon, and we're going to have a bite in town. If you think I'm afraid of being alone here, you're wrong."

"You're sure?"

"Loren, I've had a long time to think what I would do if I met those men again."

She spoke the words in an expressionless way.

"Uh-huh. What would you do?"

"Don't let's talk about it."

She stared at me unfeelingly as I kissed her on the cheek and said goodbye again. She worried me a lot.

I drove to the Tremorne Street gas station and filled up. I bought a pack of chicken salad sandwiches for my lunch, a TV dinner, and a bottle of orange juice from the convenience store. As I headed the car toward the highway, my spirits lifted – two tranquil days ahead, and all quiet on the Chadwin front. I would settle down, and come back to Greg and the twins like my old self.

I entered 'Pine Hill', leaving the front door open. The air was still, and warm compared to Cedar Falls. The house needed fresh air. I followed my routine of opening windows, and then going to the kitchen and fixing a coffee. I sat down by the window in the thinking seat. My cherished simple life was weighed down by Chadwin, but there was a possibility that as a result of our last conversation, he would abandon his pursuit of me. And there was Greg's certainty that despite Eve Chadwin's haughty disdain of me, she would have given her husband hell. It would all help. These possibilities, and the knowledge that I was packing to leave anyway, expanded warmly, and absorbed me in a reverie.

I was interrupted by a noise, a creak of the dry timber floor under the weight of a person. It could have been the house, which is constructed of timber on the upper floor, flexing itself in the sun, and the wind. I listened. Nothing, except the sighing of the pine forest. I began to relax again.

As I turned my head I could see, through the kitchen door, a section of the shiny cedar floor in the hallway. I thought that there was a shadow on the surface. Could somebody have entered the front door, and be standing in the hall, blocking the light? A quiver of fear and anticipation rose within me.

In a jagged moment, the imagined became real. A figure moved to fill the kitchen door-space. It was a man, with one hand resting casually on the frame, the other in the pocket of his grey slacks, grinning at me. He wore a smart tweed jacket and a light blue cashmere polo necked sweater.

7

"Hi, Loren. The door was open. I take it I didn't startle you."

I jumped to my feet. In the silence, he continued to lean casually against the door-frame, looking around, taking his time. "Nice position you've got. No trouble finding it. Eve and I fancy the Chateaugay area... I think I'll take a good look while I'm here."

My voice croaked, "You have a nerve, after what I've said to you."

"Whatever," he smiled carelessly.

I was left breathless by his effrontery. I couldn't measure a person who handle himself like this. He was outside all the bounds of propriety without seeming to have an inkling of it.

"Just remember I'm very close to keeping the promise I made," I said.

It would take the police half an hour on an emergency call, and Chadwin probably knew this.

"I thought we ought to talk. Understand each other. Like reasonable people. That's what you want, isn't it?" he shrugged, making his plump features look miserable.

"We've talked. I've said all that I can say. The only thing we can do now is to understand how it works out in practice!"

I fixed my eyes on a blue jay on the lawn without really seeing it. I had to deal with Chadwin, get him out of my life. I couldn't let what had happened in the past hang in the air above us, a deadweight like a packing case swinging from a faulty crane, a load that might crash down and shatter my life at any moment. There had to be an understanding. The past had to be stashed away by agreement – forever. Chadwin might be over-indulged, and primitively chauvinistic, but he was also smart, and the one redeeming glimmer in his present intrusion was that he at least seemed ready to listen.

Although I was apprehensive about Chadwin because of the uncertainty of what he might do, I felt I was stronger than him. My strength was the knowledge of the wrong he had done, which he must know, however much he rationalised and diminished it. I loathed him, and while I was alarmed by his peculiar behaviour, I had no physical fear of him. I had suffered the ultimate pain years ago in the back of his car, in the courthouse, and with poor Grace afterwards. Beneath my outward apprehensions, there was a metallic hardness in my belly about all of this. I had made my decision. I was clear. I had been forced to empty my problems over Greg like a bucket of slops, but I wouldn't shrink now from trying to settle with Chadwin. I launched into him.

"I want things to be crystal clear between us. I want your promise to keep away from me. I'll make the same promise to you. I'm the woman you raped."

My tone was frigid but level, and Chadwin looked at me patronisingly.

"Right. Right. You've said your piece. I drive all this way for five minutes of your time?"

He looked out at the darkening sky through the kitchen window, considering his response. He shook his golden head in rejection.

"Now I'm going to have my say. I'm going to screw you Loren. I'm going to redress the balance for Yonkers. And for you and your wimp of a husband blabbing to my wife. A goddam good screw. It's what you deserve. It's what you want. It's what you need. And it's what you're going to get."

I was paralysed. I couldn't feel my feet on the floor. I was sure he meant it. In a few seconds, he had cast me back fifteen years to the rear seat of the Chevrolet Bel-Air.

"Are you going to break my jaw too?"

"I don't want to hurt you. It's up to you."

"You better think again. My husband will be here soon."

"Marty told me your husband is going to see his folks in Baltimore this weekend," he smirked.

"What have you been saying to him about me?"

"Marty even suggested I drop by here when he knew I was interested in getting a place. He thinks Eve and I would enjoy the lake. We talked about the area. I'll be seeing the Kutashs later. Marty's going to show me around."

"Don't you care about the police?"

He brought the broad palms of his hands up with a flash of amusement. "What can they do? You know me. You've been fucked by me. You invite me up here. We start to make love. You change your mind. What will the cops say? Not much."

"You're scum."

"Words won't do it, Loren."

I began to sweat. I was running with moisture, yet cold. I had to get out of the house, into the woods, make my way to the nearest cabin. I'd been wrong about Chadwin. He wasn't merely looking for an erotic thrill, but for an unconscionable revenge. I persisted in appealing to reason; there was nothing else I could do.

"Don't you care about your reputation? You've come to a big job at Hudson. You have your wife..."

"Don't *you* care about *your* reputation?" he snarled.

My resentment boiled, but I had to keep control of myself. He seemed to be gambling that I would cave in. I was calculating the chance of getting past him to the door, and thinking at the same time that he could easily outrun me.

"Is there anything to eat here?" he asked suddenly, in a mild and pleasant voice.

I saw this could be my opportunity to get into a more favourable position to escape. I turned to the tray on which I had placed the chicken sandwiches and orange juice.

"Anything stronger?" Chadwin asked picking up the glass of juice.

"Nothing in the house," I lied.

A couple of crates of good claret and cabernet sauvignon lay in the workshop, and there was whiskey in the lounge.

"No frills, huh? Where's the nearest store?"

"A short way along the road," I lied.

"A friendly neighbour?"

"There are houses in the trees a few yards away," I lied.

"I think we'll forgo the booze on this occasion. Is this cold chicken, or cold turkey?" Chadwin asked, with a spurt of laughter, pointing at the sandwich.

I must have radiated a chill which killed his attempt at a joke.

"Let's go through to the lounge. Show me your hidey-hole," he said.

Chadwin took the tray and my upper arm firmly, and pushed me ahead of him. When he saw the patio overlooking the lake, he made me slide open the glass door, and shoved me through. He followed. Clouds had blotted out the sun. Lake Chateaugay was as level and grey as a slab of slate. Chadwin put the tray on a table and slid the door closed. Then he threw himself down in a deck-chair, and began to wolf the sandwich. I was imprisoned on the patio with him. The only way out, unless I threw myself into the lake, was the way we had come in. As for the lake, granite boulders protruded from the shallows twenty feet below the patio.

"Have some," Chadwin said, pointing to the untouched half of the sandwich.

"I'd be sick."

Chadwin's eyes flickered at me threateningly. He looked round like a dog sniffing out a new patch. He nodded in appreciation, his mouth full of food.

"Just what Eve and I are looking for. You wouldn't mind me as a neighbour, would you?"

I squatted awkwardly on the edge of a chair, quickly deciding that I had to talk until I had an opportunity to escape. I seethed under Chadwin's insults, but I stifled my feelings. If I pressed too hard now, or went to pieces, I would hasten the performance of Chadwin's threat. I still had a hard resolve in me. I would talk, and bank on the hope, which now seemed remote, that there was at least a wafer-thin crust of mercy over Chadwin's libidinous inferno – *and* I would be vigilant for a lapse in his attention.

Chadwin wasn't a conversationalist, but I prodded him into a rambling monologue. It seemed that he only read the financial columns, but I was at home there. He touched on the Dow, Federal Reserve policy, and Hudson's prospects. It was incredible to me that I could be listening to this trite talk against the background of his threat. Indeed, it was hard to realise that this petty-minded man could have made such a threat. He seemed, at this moment, drably sane.

Chadwin shied away from talk about his second wife. "Eve doesn't understand me," was her cliched epitaph. He begrudged his wife the fact that she was well off, and had family links with board members of Hudson. On balance, I gathered Eve was an asset like his houses, his stock portfolio, and his pension fund. He said his previous marriage had been to a stupid bitch. His kid was with his first wife. Both were a load of trouble, always milking him.

Chadwin was not curious about me. The only subject he really warmed to, was himself. He could lick most twenty-year olds at tennis, he said. His squash was state championship standard, and he played golf on a handicap of four. He reckoned he was set fair to become CEO of Hudson before long.

"We might even take your company over, Loren," he added, with satisfaction.

"It helps having a wife who owns a cut of Hudson," I said, the words crawling irresistibly out of my mouth.

"Are you kidding?" he replied, his pink face reddening. "I don't need any fucking help from her!"

There wasn't a lot to Dwight Loughlin Chadwin II. He was a large, healthy, good-looking athlete. He had been programmed. His enjoyments appeared to be sex, sport, food and drink, and work, probably in that order. He was privileged by his education and marriage. He had social poise and confidence. All this, with an ape-like insensitivity. He was self-centred to the point of blindness, and stiflingly uninteresting. And yet, if I looked at what he had said to me, literally, since he had arrived in Cedar Falls, he was seriously unhinged. On one hand, he presented as a shallow and egotistical sensualist, on another as a misanthrope who had no regard for human feelings or the law. He plainly had no respect for women. He was the kind of man who would stand aside to let a woman pass through a doorway first, but in his lexicon, women were for sex, for looking after the house and kids, and bringing assets into the family. They weren't people or friends, like the guys in the locker room.

I had steered Chadwin's talk into a safe harbour of superficial politeness, the business and sports small talk, with a glutinous overlay of sexual innuendo, which was his staple chatter. But his paltry thoughts were becoming threadbare, and the action he threatened had to follow soon. I was being impelled, powerless, toward a precipice.

8

I decided to try to stall Chadwin further by talking about the past. Perhaps if I needled him a little he would take time to justify himself.

"You didn't even get a conviction, did you? Community service. Suspended sentence. Right?"

"Right into the big subject, hey? I cut some hedges for the Parks Department."

"You sure had one smart lawyer. Do you realise the harm you did to me and my sister?"

"That's the way it was," Chadwin said, waving his hand as though he wasn't the cause.

I had a vivid memory of the snotty young college man, with his neat hair and tailor-made suit, the rising sportsman, the hero of the graduation ball, with his outriders smoothing his path, the adoring girls, the parents, the lawyers, cops and judges.

"Just a harmless prank," I said.

"Hell, that was the intention. We didn't go out looking for girls so we could hurt them. Goddam, we didn't even go out looking for girls. We picked you up in the old Chevvy Bel-Air. You were hitching with another girl."

"My sister. We weren't hitching."

"The Bel-Air was Duane's. Beautiful cruiser. Looked like a damn juke box. Duane's dead."

I couldn't curb a beat of satisfaction about Duane Schultz, although the only vision I had had of him was as a wild animal. "What happened?"

"Auto wreck. Spun his Aston Martin on Interstate 90. Got splayed by a rig. Must be five years ago. A nice guy, Duane."

Chadwin paused, thinking of his friend, but I was unmoved and silent.

"We were cruising, just chilling out, we passed you two. We stopped and offered you."

Chadwin was more relaxed now, lying back, his jacket off, his eyes fixed on a gleaming sliver of lake lit by a ray of sun which had pierced the cloud.

"It was Yonkers. You stopped on Clement Street. A row of factories. We were on the sidewalk. You guys hustled us into the car, right?"

"You agreed. We didn't beat you over the head, or push you into the car."

"It was Saturday. Nobody around. You stopped in the street, and both got out, and came over to us, and gave us a lot of bullshit, and shoved us into the car."

"Maybe," Chadwin allowed.

"And we said you had to let us out at the Dane Avenue Supermarket, and you agreed, but you didn't do that."

"I don't recollect," Chadwin said, grudgingly.

"That's what happened."

"Hell, we didn't think you were so keen to go to the supermarket or wherever."

"So?"

"So we drove somewheres to neck, and I don't recall you protesting too much."

"We did protest. We didn't scream. We thought you'd pull over."

Chadwin gave a shrug of doubt.

The uncertainties of that meeting were still clear to me. First, the ride with a couple of pushy young men, stylishly groomed, well spoken, the sort you'd expect would help an old man cross the road, or call the milkman sir. Then our attempts to get them to stop the car in Dane Avenue, low key to start, but near hysterical as the men joked, made to pull over, and then didn't. And then realising that the car was heading out of town, and knowing what these males had in mind, but still believing that two such apparently refined young men wouldn't force anything.

"You drove to Kiverton Park. A new subdivision of building lots with roads finished, but all the sites bare, except for a few trees. Deserted."

I could see it as starkly as yesterday. I could smell old leather seats, and the after-shave. Chadwin gave me his shiny-eyed, healthy-boy smile.

"You told us you lived in Tarrytown."

"Yeah, you didn't have to be worried about doing dirt on the daughters of friends from the Scarsdale Country Club."

I had mentioned where Grace and I lived in innocence, but it was received as a piece of information which set us apart. The two men batted Tarrytown back and forwards between themselves in the car with knowing winks. They had captured a couple of bimbos from Tarrytown. That was where the Greeks and Italians and Polacks who worked at the Chrysler plant at Stony Creek lived, in tenements. In their eyes, Grace and I were down-market, and likely to be less fussy about whom we screwed with. This piece of information about us gave Chadwin and Schultz confidence. They had carefree lives, and were going exciting places. Grace and I were there to help it happen.

The men had stilled our calls to be let out of the car with hilarity, promises, and mock sincerity. It was a circus performance that left us – I keep saying us – but I mean me – just short of panic, but still with the belief that we would be released. Shultz had parked the scarlet and white monster under the trees, off the road. Grace was beside Duane in the front. I remembered that sitting in the back of the car I was thinking that we were heading into something I had only read about in the Sunday newspapers. Chadwin's body against mine had been like an uncomfortably shaped piece of metal, except that he had a soft wet mouth, a minty breath and polished, even teeth.

I don't know when the point came that I realised that this wasn't bluff by the men, and wasn't going to stop. The leather richness of Chadwin's jacket as he had slipped it off had stifled me. I tried to scream. Chadwin gagged me by covering my mouth with his.

"I told you then by every signal one human being can send to another that I didn't want you."

Chadwin mused, eyes on the bright distance, the edge of the dark cloud layer over the forest. "I thought you were playin' around."

"And I told you and Duane about my sister, that she couldn't speak properly, and couldn't handle this situation."

"Shit, I thought that was a story."

The manhandling I received was an explosive fireball in my memory. Chadwin pummelled me as if I had been a cushion. He tore my clothes off. He plunged his fingers between my legs like ferocious burrowing lizards. I could hear Grace's screams and moans, and Duane Schultze's curses as he grappled with her.

"You bit my tongue. You hurt me in the goddamnedist place, and I slapped you," Chadwin protested as though he was fully justified.

He had roared and thrown me off. His balled fist smashed the side of my nose. Another fist struck my jaw and I felt it snap like a bar of sugar candy.

"You punched hell out of me!"

"I lost my temper. I didn't mean it. I don't beat up on women."

"You don't?" I said in a dead voice. "You left me with broken bones, and the marks, and the memory."

"Christ! If you hadn't bitten me!"

The car was full of wrenching sobs and masculine curses that day when the men's excursion into pleasure was over. I was only partly conscious of what had happened to Grace, but she could put up no resistance. The car became suddenly quieter; only tortured breathing, and Grace's keening, and Schultz telling her to shut up. He pulled out a bottle of Scotch whisky from the glove compartment. He uncorked it, had a slug, and passed the bottle to Chadwin. When Chadwin had drunk and passed the bottle back to him, Schultz grabbed a handful of Grace's hair, forced the neck of the bottle into her mouth, and poured. She choked.

Chadwin thought it was a joke. He snatched the bottle from Schultz and tried the same with me. I screamed with pain from my jaw. The neck of the bottle split my lips. Chadwin's temper flared again at the resistance, and he poured whisky over my head as I sat coughing whisky and blood.

I don't remember pulling on my torn clothes. Schultz started up the car and drove for a few miles. Grace seemed numb. Chadwin swigged at what was left of the whisky. The men pushed us out of the car at a vacant lot between two factories near the Mill River Tollway. We collapsed on the ground, and the car blasted away, its stereo system blaring. We were sprawled in the dust, unable at first even to feel the full effect of our injuries. But the pain advanced quickly, and I realised we both needed hospital treatment urgently.

Getting help that day was a different kind of nightmare. Nobody was about. The buildings around us were closed, empty. I had tried to stop one of the few passing cars, but they honked furiously at the dishevelled woman who waved so frantically at them, swerved, and drove on. In desperation I stepped in front of a car and held up both arms. It squealed to a halt. As soon as I came close to the driver's window, he yelled "bitch!" and stepped on the gas.

I knew that Grace and I looked alarming. My nose had bled, and my lips and chin were covered with blood. My blouse buttons had been ripped off. The waistband of my skirt was broken. Grace's thin dress was torn at the neck. We probably looked like a couple of drug-crazies, rather than women in trouble. And my jaw had an aching numbness which was creeping up my face.

We were alone in one of those places which seems ordered and benign, but is actually a desert. Beyond the vacant lot where we had been dumped, there were a number of low rise modern factories, with neat lawns and flower beds in front, empty parking lots, and wide, well-paved, deserted sidewalks. I saw a car parked by the front office of one factory, and I crossed the parking lot and the grass to get there. I knocked at the door and there was a movement behind the glass. A security guard, his belt sagging with keys, emerged.

"Whaddya want?" he asked suspiciously.

I couldn't speak at first. I tried to say we'd been attacked, and wanted to report to the police and see a doctor. The words didn't come out clearly. The guard looked down on me from the doorway. He was a rock-faced, shaven-headed man of sixty. His look said he'd seen it all. He shook his head negatively.

"You've had a mite too much to drink it looks to me."

He didn't believe the ragged, bloodstained, whisky-smelling girl. He pointed to the road, where the folorn figure of Grace waited.

"Get offa the property, and get your ass someplace else!"

I dragged the crying Grace with me along the bare sidewalks, until I found a callbox after half a mile. I made an emergency call, and we sat in the gutter and waited. In fifteen minutes a patrol cruiser arrived, with a big moustached old cop who took his time with the questions. I said we'd been taken in a car, raped, beaten up, and dumped. The cop made notes, leaning on the bonnet of the black and white, as coolly as if he was dealing with a stop light violation.

"I think my jaw is broken," I said.

The cop must have seen the swelling, and the shadow of bleeding under the skin.

"What about her?" the cop asked, pointing at Grace.

"She can understand, but she can't respond."

"You girls been drinkin'?"

At that point I passed out, and the cop was left with a mute, and a body.

I woke up in the emergency ward of the Hampton Hospital, screens around my bed. I could hear voices, cries of pain. My face was bandaged. A wire brace was fixed on my neck to keep my jaw in place. My mouth was burning and seemed to be full of poisonous chemicals.

A nurse looked round the screen. "Hi there! Ready to talk to the police yet?"

"How is my sister?" I managed to spit out.

The nurse didn't answer. I guessed the man standing behind the nurse was a cop. He was in a grey suit, with a white shirt, and tie, and he held a notebook. He had a sceptical stare like the guard at the factory.

"Detective Moran. I understand you say you were assaulted and raped?" he said, drawing up a chair beside the bed.

"And my sister."

I told him my story haltingly.

"The patrolman who brought you in says you'd been drinking alchoholic liquor. Is that right?"

When I explained, he said, "I see," as though it was a weak excuse. I pressed him about Grace, and he said she had been referred to a psychiatric ward, and hadn't spoken.

He talked of identification of the men, and I gave him their first names, and described the car. I was also able to give most of the numbers on the New York licence plate. I had repeated those numbers over and over, as the car moved off after dumping us.

"We should get these men without too much trouble with the information you've given us, Miss Reynaud," he said, more warmly.

I noticed that another man had slipped through the screen and was listening. He was a contrast to Moran, a smart tan suit, an attractive smile, and a pile of longish grey hair.

"You can leave the lady with me," he said to Moran, taking the chair as the cop stood up. "And let me know how it goes."

"Call me," Carl Moran said, walking out without a glance at me.

"I'm Desmond Flynn," the new man said, placing a name card on the bedside table.

I shook my head, not understanding.

"I'm an attorney, at your service. I have a lot of cases representing people like you. I can help you get the damages and treatment you're entitled to."

He already seemed to know about the case. I answered his questions, and signed a paper giving him representation.

"Don't worry about a thing, my dear," Flynn said, picking up the medical notes from the file at the end of the bed, studying them professionally, and making some notes of his own on a pad.

"When you identify the attackers, we'll hang a substantial claim on them. You may need plastic surgery."

As Flynn was putting his papers in his briefcase and preparing to go, I asked him how he found me.

"Oh, I look into this ward every so often and have a cup of coffee with the ward sister."

He gave me a strong smile and I felt more at ease.

A week later I identified Dwight Chadwin and Duane Schultz from a line-up at the police precinct. I heard that they admitted they were the two after questioning. I had been in a dazed state since the rape happened. I couldn't *feel* anything. I was observing what was happening around me without being able to intervene. Flynn came to see me at home, and said he was going to make the rich daddies pay.

My father was grimly silent. I think he felt shamed personally by what had happened to his daughters. In his heart he believed Grace and I had gone willingly in the car. He thought, as the cops inferred, that we were at fault. He didn't have a wife to share his confidences, or modify his masculine impulses. He hadn't found a companion since my mother's death ten years before. He was out of work, and seldom saw his old buddies from the Stony Bend plant, where he used to be a spray-painter. He used to sit for hours in the apartment, in the dark, watching television, sipping beer, and growing a paunch. But the mention of the damages suit energised him, and he and Flynn spent time talking about how much money was in issue.

I met prosecuting attorney Bronstein at the District Attorney's office, and he echoed the scepticism of the police. The only thing that seemed to impress him favourably was the medical evidence that both Grace and I had been virgins before the attack.

A few weeks after the disaster of the court hearing, Desmond Flynn called at the apartment and talked to my father. They were together half an hour. Then my father called me in and told me to sign a document settling my claim for $5,000. Although I felt this was wrong, my father and Flynn insisted. Flynn had changed his tune, but not his jovial plausibility.

"Sign and take the money while you can, my dear girl. It's a good settlement. There's a lot of dispute about what happened, and you might do worse in court."

"I don't mind going to court," I protested.

"Ah, yes, but that costs a lot of money. These families are big politically, and they'll fight. I can't work for free," Flynn said.

I asked about Grace's money, and Flynn said he was dealing with that for a similar amount. So I signed the form. The case was over, but not the pain.

The sun had broken through more strongly at Chateaugay, and painted the far end of the lake a glaring white.

"Did you ever hear of a lawyer named Desmond Flynn? He was the ambulance chaser who added me to his client list in the emergency ward, and filed a suit for damages."

"That kinda thing was handled by my father," Chadwin said wearily.

"Yeah, well he did a job. The money we got was derisory."

"You want money now?"

"Don't be like that. I'm just telling you."

I hadn't moved Chadwin any closer to understanding the consquences of his acts because all the forces around him had moved to soften the effects. He had no idea of the harm that had been done to Grace. When she came out of hospital, the only person she felt at ease with was me. My father didn't understand, almost resented a disabled daughter. He used to stare silently at her with eyes that were deep in their sockets of worry.

I knew I would have to look after Grace, and I planned to get a job in Trenton, NJ and take her with me. I wanted to get away from my father, from his personal misery and self pity, and from the reproachful way he treated us, two soiled women. Grace resumed her domestic work at the apartment, while I worked as a trainee secretary at the Lindos plant, which made steel pressings for General Motors. At the same time I was studying accountancy at night, and making plans to move to Trenton. I was going with a girlfriend from Lindos. We were going to share an apartment, with Grace to look after us. In this period at home before we were ready to move, Grace became silent, haunted.

One night I came home at quarter to seven as usual. My father wasn't there. He usually hung around the local pool hall until eight. This was a time when I could spend some leisure with Grace, doing things in the apartment together, helping with the cooking, talking a little.

As soon as I let myself in I knew something was wrong. The lights were off, the rooms in the deep shadow of surrounding buildings. There was no smell of cooking. I could hear the filtered sounds of the neighbours' children and radios. I called Grace's name and went to her bedroom. The bed was neatly made but the woolly bear which usually sat on her pillow wasn't there. I thought she'd run away. And then I heard an unusual sound. Water running. Not the neighbours' plumbing. Yes, it was running water. The bathroom door was in front of me. I pushed it open. All I could see for a moment was that the bath was full of black water. The tap was on, and water was running through the overflow vent. I switched on the light to see Grace's naked body under blood red water, and the teddy bear floating on the surface.

"God, that's awful," Chadwin said. "I didn't know that, but you can't blame me."

The word-pictures were dim and distant for him.

"Yes, you are to blame. She was over six months pregnant, and she miscarried in the emergency unit."

Chadwin considered this for a moment, surprised, and then dismissed it. "OK, sure. Like you say."

He rose from the chair, stretching and yawning, a beast preparing to move. I stood up with a cold realisation that the moment had come. He wasn't used to accounting for anything outside the prosaic responsibilities of business, and he wasn't used to being held up by a woman.

"Now let's seal our little chat with a friendly kiss," he simpered, stepping toward me, clamping his large hands on my upper arms. He held me tight at arm's length.

"Oh, come on, Loren. You've got a neurosis about all this. It's like I said. You won't admit what you really want. And it'll be therapeutic. It'll release all the shit that's blocking you up. And you owe me one for all the grief you've caused."

He was drawing me toward him, the puce face, the shark teeth, the flaring gold hair, the silver eyes. Instead of calming him, the nauseating story had stimulated him. He was throbbing. He crushed my mouth and breasts and thighs to him.

9

I didn't resist Chadwin when he grabbed me. I didn't speak. I had said everything to him. Words could not save me. I didn't cry out. Nobody would hear me. My veins had turned to bile. I had to change my tactic completely to avoid Chadwin carrying me inside, and throwing me on a bed. I had to give myself an opportunity to overcome his physical strength.

"OK, maybe you're right. I'm hung up," I said, weakly.

"You surely are, kid," he gasped.

"Look, let's go inside."

"Yeah, do it properly," he breathed, sliding the patio door, and thrusting me through.

"If you'll give me a chance, I'll get us a drink. I've remembered, there is a bottle of bourbon."

"Holding out on me, huh?"

"Not any more. Just let me go, so I can get it."

"I knew you'd see sense. You're a smart girl."

He followed me closely while I fished the bottle out of the lounge cabinet, poured hefty slugs, and fetched ice from the freezer, and put it in a bucket.

"Now you're being a nice girl," he said, ramming his body close to me from behind while I mixed the drinks, pawing my breasts, working himself up.

I was thinking that the bottle might be a weapon, if I could get into the right position to swing it. And there was a baseball bat, which Greg and the twins used to play with, in the clothes closet, in the hall. I could not get to the bat while Chadwin was shadowing my every step. The kitchen drawer was full of knives, but I wasn't confident enough with them. Chadwin might turn the knife on me.

"The bedroom's through here," I said, walking ahead with the bottle, two glasses and the ice-bucket on a tray.

I led him to the spare bedroom. The bed, where I had intended to sleep later, was made up with pale blue sheets.

"Very inviting," Chadwin said, dropping his jacket on a chair, and slurping his drink heavily, but making sure I didn't get out of reach, by blocking my way.

"Let me go to the bathroom for a moment, will you?"

"I'll be waiting outside."

I went into the ensuite room. There was nothing in here in the way of a weapon except surgical scissors; but the sharp points scared me. I looked at myself in the mirror; a woman with a waxen face, a mussed ponytail, and sweat glistening below the hairline. If there was another way to deal with this man, I couldn't think of it. I used the perfume atomiser automatically, let my hair loose, and brushed it a couple of times.

"What in hell are you doing, Loren? Taking it out of mothballs?" Chadwin yelled.

"Pig!" I said under my breath, and went out. "Let me get you another drink."

Chadwin's bad-tempered glare melted when he saw my hair, and smelt me. "Hey, you are something, baby."

He followed closely while I refilled his glass, unable to wait. "C'mon, before I die."

His lust was so overpowering that he could believe that somebody who had expressed only repulsion toward him, could now enjoy him. I put the bottle back on the tray which rested on the table by the bed. Now wasn't the moment to try to hit him. Not while he was on his feet. Chadwin pushed me towards the bed, kicking off his shoes and trousers, and unbuttoning his shirt. I was calculating how I could pick up the bottle by the neck and get a clear swing at him.

Chadwin gulped the whole drink, put down the glass, and fell on the bed, pulling me down with him. I was engulfed by his thickly muscled red gold arms and his hard body. He rolled on top of me, writhing, his lips and tongue wetting my face. I retreated into an inner darkness. He was pushing and grunting and thrusting at me, but it was all happening out there, in parts of me I hardly owned. I writhed with hatred. Chadwin took my agony for passion. His urge for self-satisfaction was so strong that I might as well have been a plastic doll – or a corpse.

He was tearing at my clothes, groaning, fumbling between my legs like a pastrycook kneading dough. His open eyes were blind. He uttered the first poetic words of this close encounter.

"I want it, baby, real bad!"

His filthy grunting only strengthened my resolve. He reared up, kneeling between my legs, intending to pull my jeans and pants off. I was free, for a second, to reach out for the whiskey bottle beside the bed. Chadwin's movements were so aggressive, that my arm jerked as I tried to close my fingers over the neck of the bottle. The bottle crashed to the floor, taking the tray, glasses and ice-bucket with it. Chadwin only laughed, thinking I was throwing my arms about in ecstasy. The bottle – my prospective weapon – had come to rest on its side a yard from the bed. He read the pain on my face as pleasure.

When Chadwin moved to one side of my legs to drag my jeans down, his weight was off me for a moment, and I thrust myself sideways, out of the bed, falling on to the floor, and felt fragments of broken glass stab into my hands and feet.

"Whatinhell?" Chadwin said, befuddled for a moment.

I reached across the floor, and grabbed the neck of the bottle. I reared up on my knees. Chadwin was still half lying on the bed. I hit him across the ear with the bottle, but he merely shook his head.

"Fucking hell!" he shouted, an arm up to protect himself.

I fell back on the floor. I had missed my chance. Chadwin threw himself off the bed, towards me, his throat swelled with bellows of fury; but the fury turned into a cry of agony. He had stamped his foot down on the base of a broken whiskey glass. Sharp slivers of crystal, sticking up from the base, had stabbed into his foot. He reared back in pain, sitting on the floor. He looked helplessly at the knives of glass buried deep in his flesh. I jumped up, and swung the bottle at him again. The bottle connected with his head. Again he shook his head, confused for a few seconds. I was fired up now. I wasn't afraid. I was going to fight the bastard, and give him what he gave me in the back of the Bel Air.

"You mad bitch!" he shouted, reaching out for me, clamping a hand on one of my ankles and drawing me toward him, trying to drag me down.

He attempted to protect his head by pulling me close to him. I rammed the base of the bottle down on the crown of his head. He released his hold a little, groggy. I tore myself away. I had a chance now to aim the bottle hard at him, like a club. It exploded on his forehead, spraying glass and the remains of the bourbon everywhere. Chadwin's arms dropped, and he flopped back on the floor.

I ran out of the room, grabbed the baseball bat from the hall alcove, and went back. Chadwin was groaning, hoisting himself up on his elbows. I had a measured swing at him with the bat. It struck the side of his head, over his ear, with a bony thunk. He went down, unconscious.

I only spent a moment looking at the blood and glass around us, and at Chadwin's limp body. I ran out of the bedroom, and downstairs to the workshop. I feared that if Chadwin came to, and had a chance to get at me, he'd beat me to pulp as well as rape me. I took two coils of plastic cord off the pegs above the workbench. Greg used the cord, which was strong enough to tow a car, on the sailboats, and he had taught me how to tie sailors' knots. I ran back upstairs. Chadwin was on his side. I turned him on to his belly with difficulty. I trussed his wrists together behind his back first; then his ankles. He was becoming conscious, moaning. For additional security, I bent his legs, and tied his ankles to his wrists with the surplus cord. He was like a turkey ready for roasting.

"I'm going to kill you, you murderous bitch," he slurred.

I didn't believe that. He'd only do the next worst thing. I backed away from him, satisfied that I was safe for the moment. The room reeked of whisky and blood and the French perfume I had squirted on my hair. I closed the door. I had survived.

I ran into the kitchen, and clutched the telephone to ring the police and Greg. The line was dead. I pressed the buttons on the phone. Silence. I went through to the phone in the dining room, but it was dead too. The broadband modem next to the computer had been torn away from its connections. At some point when I was fiddling with drinks, Chadwin had taken this precaution. And at Chateaugay there was no coverage for my mobile phone.

10

Think. I had to think. I slumped in my special seat by the window. I felt tired, my limbs heavy, and aching as though I'd done a hard day's physical work. The soles of my feet prickled with the pain of the broken glass. My breasts, I could see, when I eased up my sweater, were red and blue. I had an absolute conviction that I couldn't have acted otherwise to save myself. I had a tiny, and perhaps impermanent glow of satisfaction at having triumphed, at last, over this man who had violated my life. Then I felt a weight of exhaustion, of hopelessness. I must have passed out for a few seconds, or perhaps minutes. The next sound I heard was somebody ringing the doorbell.

I came out of my chair as if I was on a spring, and went into the bedroom. Chadwin had heard the bell, and he began to shout. I pushed one of my handkerchiefs into his mouth and tied an old scarf around his head, ran back to the kitchen, and switched on the radio. It was KWTR which is mostly rock music, and I turned up the volume. I needed the police desperately, but I didn't necessarily want to involve just anybody who called at the door. I wanted time to think what to do. I wanted time to clean up the bedroom.

I could see the shape of a man in the frosted glass of the front door as I went through the hall. He was wearing a county official's wide-brimmed felt hat.

"Hold it a minute!" I yelled.

I went into the main bedroom, and took my bloody jeans and sweater off and slipped into an old green velour track-suit.

It took only a few moments to do that. By the time I got to the door, the visitor was walking away. I could have kept quiet and let him go, but there was a chance he could help me.

"Sorry to keep you. Just doing a bit of cleaning, you know," I said loudly as I opened the door.

"That's all right lady," the man said, turning, and I recognised the pest control badge, with the name 'Earl Rovnik' stitched on it. He was the rat-catcher, and not exactly a figure of authority who could relieve my cares.

"I'm working round here now, and I thought you might like the loan of these," he said, holding up two traps.

I told him I'd leave the trapping to him.

"I'll be hereabouts a while, and you'll end up good and clean."

"How did you know I was here?"

He pointed down toward the forecourt. "Saw your husband come past a while back. Always notice them fancy foreign cars."

Chadwin's Jaguar stood in front of the garages.

I thanked him, and he paused as he turned away. He was looking at my right hand. "You hurt yourself bad, lady?"

My hand was bright with blood.

"Snagged it in the workshop. Nothing really."

I closed the door, and saw him walk slowly away. I leaned on the door for the moment. I could have told him what happened. I could have handed Chadwin over to him. But I was still confused. And wary. I was worried about the liquor and perfume in the bedroom. The radio was racketing so loudly I couldn't think.

I turned down the volume. I made myself a strong cup of coffee, and sipped it without milk or sugar. I felt calmer after I'd finished the drink. It was very obvious that I couldn't simply release Chadwin, and hope he'd go away. The man had a strange compulsion. He would have to be handed to the police, roped up, and I'd have to face an investigation, and perhaps, the way these things went, be regarded by some with suspicion. What I had to do was to lessen that possibility by cleaning up the house – the blood, the glass, the spilt liquor. I was beginning to feel more composed. I simply had to use my head. If Greg had been at home, I could have asked him to come to Chateaugay immediately, but that option wasn't open. I couldn't have called him from here anyway.

I went into Chadwin's room to check on him, the pink monster, groaning a little for breath, his eyes sticking out like marbles. I removed the scarf from his mouth; it was bloodstained. And there was blood on the sheets and the floor, but Chadwin was surviving.

He mouthed hoarsely, "I'm not afraid of cunt, baby, and when I get hold of you…"

I didn't speak to him. I couldn't address complete unreason. I put a plaster on my arm, picked the fragments of glass out of my feet, and found my slippers. I decided I'd work in the track-suit and burn it. I suddenly remembered the car out front. It immediately raised the question, where was the driver? I decided to put the car into the garage in the meantime. I got the keys from Chadwin's jacket.

When I went outside, the wind was sighing in the pines. It was a lonely sound. Occasionally a gust whistled around the house, pressing the window panes, and making the windows creak. The pine forest was like a dark sea, rolling in aggressive waves, and lapping at the windows of the house. I put the car in the garage, closed it, and locked the doors between the garage and the workshop.

I went upstairs and resumed cleaning around Chadwin. He scoffed, "I may have slapped you around a few years ago, but you could get ten to twenty for what you're doing."

"Listen, you punk. I was a kid when it happened. Since then

I've followed many cases in the newspapers. I've learned about plea bargaining. And how a woman, alone with a man, can have difficulty having her word preferred. Maybe *I'll* have to plea bargain, this time. Your word against mine. What a story!"

"The story, lady, is all over my body!" Chadwin sneered.

"Wrong again. If you were right, the scenario in the Westchester Court would have been about my beat-up face, and the doctor's report on my vagina. But they didn't count. The yarn as told by your greaseball lawyer, was about a football hero. Things haven't changed. If I'm on trial for this, it's about a criminal who plea-bargained out of rape, got a fixation on his victim, followed her to her house, terrorised her, beat her up, and tried to rape her again."

I showed him the cuts on my hands and feet, and I unzipped my tracksuit so he could see the bruises, now carmine, black and yellow, from under my brassiere, the legacy of our struggle on the bed.

"Yeah, I reckon a court will be fairly sympathetic to a family woman who puts a few bruises on the man, ties him up, and hands him over to the cops, which is what I'm going to do with you. Don't you realise that? I'm going to give you to the cops like a Thanksgiving turkey. That'll look good in the newspapers!"

It came out better than I expected, sounded quite credible. Chadwin was momentarily silenced. Even he could see that there could be another side to the story.

"Nobody is going to believe you this time around, Chadwin. Not when I've got through the telling. You'll be front page news. A turkey! How will that square with your new job, big man? They'll love you down at Hudson. And your wife'll be so proud of you when the board of directors meet!"

"You scheming, fucking bitch!"

11

I mopped the bedroom floor around Chadwin, but I couldn't get rid of the smell of whiskey and perfume. I decided not to burn the bloodstained bedclothes, or the mattress; they were evidence of the struggle. What I wanted to do was to eliminate anything, like the presence of liquor, which might suggest I was complicit with Chadwin. Whiskey poured over my head had counted against me at Westchester court as if I had been a drunk.

The doorbell rang again, before I had a chance to clear away the trash I'd removed from the bedroom and dropped in the hall. One glance down the hall suggested that the two figures out there were the Kutash pair. It couldn't have been anybody worse. They would know I was here, because they could probably see movement inside the hall. And some of the upper windows were open. I would have no alternative but to invite them in. I went into the bedrooom and gagged Chadwin. I made a careful job of closing the ill-fitting bedroom door, and turned up the volume of the rock radio again.

In the short time it took me to perform these tasks, the formidable reasons why I couldn't talk honestly to the Kutashs, confide in them, or ask for their help, came to me.

Chadwin was a new friend, or acquaintance of the Kutashs. They would be slow to believe him guilty of the kind of violence I'd suffered today. They would never stand by and see him handed to the police, tied hand and foot. I was sure that their immediate reaction would be that Chadwin was one of us and had to be released. Talk might follow, but it would be dominated by Chadwin, and the Kutashs. Both Marty and Donna were irritable people, proud of the rightness of their snap decisions. Marty had already absorbed some dirt about me from Chadwin. The Kutashs would be quick to believe that I encouraged Chadwin. Whatever the twists of any discussion, Chadwin would talk himself free. I would escape violence today, but Chadwin would be stalking me tomorrow with renewed venom.

When I opened the front door, I tried to form a barrier to entry against their leering faces.

"I'm sorry, but I have to go out now."

"What for?" Donna demanded.

"The doctor. I have to see the doctor."

"I'm sorry to hear that, dear," Donna said, as she and Marty surged past me like expected guests. Donna had a narky tightness about her mouth which suggested that whatever was going on in my house, they were going to join in. Marty thrust a full bottle of bourbon at me.

"In case you're out of juice, we brought our own."

"Didn't you hear me, Marty?" I asked.

"What are you up to, honey?" Donna cooed.

"I've got a terrible migraine."

"This is the official cure for migraine," Marty said, waving the bottle.

"You do look pale, Loren," Donna said, her eyes darting about, examining, measuring.

I glanced down at myself self-consciously, and realised that the extremity of the bruises on my chest were visible. I zipped the tracksuit to my throat.

"What on earth happened to you, dear?" Donna asked, stepping forward, and reaching for the zip.

I stopped her. "I had a fall, hit my chest on a packing case in the workshop. It looks worse than it is."

"I haven't seen it yet," Donna said.

"I'm not getting undressed."

"I don't mind," Marty chuckled.

"But I do."

"You sure you're not having bondage sessions with a dashing Jaguar salesman?" Donna joked.

That was exactly how my injuries could be viewed, now that I had given an excuse for them – the result of a perverted masochistic session. And even Chadwin, bruised and bleeding and trussed up on the floor, could be seen as a participant or a victim. I was convinced I was right in concealing everything from the Kutashs. Their involvement would only make this into a filthier scandal than it already was.

I walked after Donna into the lounge, alarmed at her reference to a Jaguar.

"Do you have anything for afternoon tea?" Donna asked, plumping on a couch.

"I've just had lunch, and in any case, I have to go out," I said, going back into the kitchen, where Marty had taken over as barman.

He had turned the radio volume down, and I turned it up. "I like the Stones," I said.

"What's for you, honey?" Marty asked.

"Nothing. As I said…"

"That noise won't do you much good."

"Marty, I'm afraid you can't stay. I'm not well. Please."

When I went back into the lounge, Donna was standing by the fireplace, a hand on her hip.

"Who's DLC?" she demanded.

She was talking to me like a tax inspector.

"I don't know."

She held something behind her back, and gave me a knowing wink. She held up a key ring with a Jaguar symbol on it, which

I must have carelessly left on the hall table. I flushed hotly at her nerve.

"Must be Greg's."

"But Greg's initials aren't DLC, Loren," she said, in a childish tone

"I fucking well know that, Donna!" I said, openly annoyed, snatching the keys, and putting them in my pocket.

"Hey, what are you two girls shouting about?" Marty said, coming in with a drink for Donna and himself.

"If I've said anything..." Donna began, with pretended innocence.

"Let's have a quick drink and go. Loren isn't feeling so good," Marty said.

"Here's a puzzle for you, Marty," Donna said. "Who drives a Jaguar and has the initials DLC?"

"I dunno... the only guy I know drives a Jaguar ... Hey, DLC!... So?"

"A friend of yours, Loren?" Donna asked. "Not that I need to ask."

"Sure," Marty said.

"I think we better go," Donna said. "We could be interrupting something."

Donna threw her drink down her throat, hooted and walked to the door, followed by Marty. I was really an onlooker. I had no idea how to explain Chadwin's keys. As she flounced along, I saw that Donna noticed the bucket, and pile of bloodstained rags and broken glass which I had hurriedly swept up. I had pushed the trash into the open alcove space in the hall. Her eyes were like searchlights.

"Still cleaning up, dear?" she said.

"I didn't know you kept a dog," Marty said, as he reached the front door.

I looked at him. "A dog?"

"Yeah, I could hear it in the kitchen."

"Oh, have fun with your puppy," Donna said, widening her eyes in amusement.

"The wind often whistles in the trees as though it was a cat or a dog crying," I said, my voice trailing away hopelessly.

When I shut the door on them, I almost screamed with disappointment. The Kutashs were the last people I wanted to take into my confidence, but I had been forced into a heap of lies to avoid it.

Chadwin was suddenly making a lot of noise from the bedroom. His gag had evidently come loose. He was also banging with his feet. I went into the bedroom. I was taken aback to see that he had managed to unpick the cords that held his wrists to his ankles. And he had worked to loosen but not quite free his ankles. All that remained were his wrists. He let out an animal moan when he saw me, and hopped toward me, perhaps intending to use his feet as weapons.

"I'm going to kill you, you whore!" he said, thickly.

I bolted out of the room, and slammed the door. But it had no lock. I stumbled down the stairs to the garage three at a time, and went into the workshop, hiding behind, and partly in an empty packing case. My plan to hand a trussed-up, would-be rapist to the police had failed.

I heard Chadwin at the top of the stairs, his breath rasping, mumbling incoherently. He came down the stairs slowly, his progress impeded by his wounded foot, and his tied arms. He stopped in the workshop, presumably looking for an implement to assist in untying his wrists; that would be his priority. I was shielded from his view by the boats and the packing case, and was able to slip upstairs. It would take a time before Chadwin could dislodge one of the tools from the rack above the workbench, and use it. I locked the door at the top of the stairs, and dragged a small table across the doorway.

I went into the kitchen, and picked up the useless phone without thinking. My precautions wouldn't hold Chadwin for long. He'd soon loose his wrists. He had the option of forcing the door between the workshop and the garage. A man with both hands free, and the selection of tools available to him, would be able to do that without much trouble. If he broke out through the garage door, or the workshop door on the lakeside, he would have a number of ways of forcing entry to the house – the front door, the sundeck, the patio, the bathroom windows; all were vulnerable if you were determined.

All I could do was run down the road, and hope to flag a passing car. I wondered whether I could get my car out of the garage without the serious risk of confronting Chadwin. I was afraid he meant to carry out his threat, to the extent of harming me grievously. I went outside to the garage door and listened. I heard a knocking sound. If Chadwin caught me in the house, it would be a short and terrifying siege, with only one result. The closet in the main bedroom held a couple of shotguns, but it would take time to get one out, find the ammunition; and I would never be able to remember how to load and fire, without having time to play around.

As I re-entered the house, like a big beast, the rat-catcher's yellow van rolled slowly past, and stopped. Without a thought, except that I had to get to him, I ran across to the road, waving frantically.

"Please help me, Mr Rovnik!"

Rovnik swung out of the cab of the van slowly, smiling in a friendly way. "Hi there, Mrs Stamford. You got trouble again?"

"Oh, sure I have," I said, putting out my arms toward him

"Hey now, no need to cry," he said, putting an arm protectively around my shoulders.

"There's a man in the house, a madman who's going to kill me! Help me please!"

I suppose to a man who works mostly alone, out-of-doors with only trees and animals for company, this must have sounded slightly mad.

"You sure of that, mam?" Rovnik asked, holding me away, and examining me with a lopsided sparkle in his eye.

"Help me, take me in your van to the nearest telephone, please!"

He shrugged uncertainly, smoothed his hand over his tanned head to catch a few hairs blowing in the wind, and reached into the cab for his stetson.

"I'm shorta time, Mrs Stamford. I have a bit of work to do. I'm late now, finishing up round here. Due back at the County yard."

"Have you possibly got a gun, Mr Rovnik?"

"It's not like that, is it?"

"I might need a gun for protection."

"Why don't we call the cops?"

"Because this man cut the phone line. That's why I want you to take me."

"Tell me, mam, it's not your husband who's in there, is it?"

Rovnik had assumed that the Jaguar was my husband's car, and it wasn't in evidence any more.

"God, no! It's the guy who assaulted me!"

"Is it the feller you elbowed out last week?"

I shook my head, no. Now Rovnik would possibly think I was some kind of neurotic honey-pot.

"Wait a minute, Mrs Stamford. This guy is inside?"

"Yes, locked down in the workshop. All I want you to do is to help me call the police. At least take me with you, when you've finished your work. I don't think he'll try anything if you're with me."

Rovnik summed this up, and seemed eased by the thought that there need be no physical confrontation. And I think he only half-believed me anyway. He gave me his deep, wrinkled grin and said, "Maybe we ought to go inside first."

We went back to the house. I locked and chained the front door when we went in, and took Rovnik to the barricaded workshop door. "He's down there."

"He's not going to get through there in a hurry," Rovnik said.

There was no sound from the workshop. Rovnik listened. He eased. He looked at me with a light in his eye. He was wondering if I was telling the truth, and perhaps I did look slightly crazed. I couldn't help thinking of the time when Grace and I had been dumped on a vacant lot by Chadwin and Schultz, and nobody would believe we were victims.

"Have you got a drink, Mrs Stamford? Maybe we both need one to steady us."

I thought he was out of order, but I had to play along. I fetched a bottle of Jim Beam from the cabinet in the lounge and poured him a shot. He was beginning to see the potential in the situation.

"You not having one, Mrs Stamford?"

"I told you, I want to get out of here immediately."

"Hey, this is the way I like it," Rovnik said, easing down on the couch without any invitation.

Rovnik was treating my call for help as an indication that I was interested in him; that I had dreamed up a tale to get his attention. He didn't think there was a maniac on the loose. But for the moment at least I felt safe.

Rovnik took the bourbon fast. I listened for sounds of Chadwin. Silence in the house. Outside, the wind had dropped and the trees were still.

"I want you to drive me in to Clayburg now, this moment,

or somewhere I can make a call to the police. Will you please do that, Mr Rovnik?"

"Sure," he said, "but how about another little drink first?"

Then I was startled by a footfall on the porch, and the doorbell.

I made Rovnik come into the hall with me, and he took the opportunity to grope my ass. I could see though the frosted glass that it was a woman caller, and I opened the chained door on Donna Kutash. She had a skin like a Sherman tank. Her suspicious curiosity had completely overcome any hurt feeling she may have had as a result of my earlier rebuff to her and her husband. I was blunt.

"I'm busy, Donna."

"My," she said, taking no notice of me.

She looked past me, down the hall and saw Rovnik. "All locked up cosy. Having a private party?"

She walked in. Donna's eyes were measuring, checking, adding two and two and making six. She was looking at Rovnik. Under her anorak, I could see she had changed to a pink lurex sweater shot with silver thread. She had added dangly earrings and plenty of war-paint. She was going to party.

I was safe enough if Donna was about, but to try to explain the situation to her, so I could get *her* instead of Rovnik to take me to the police, was just too much to face. Donna would interrogate me like a spy. She'd help me, but she'd want to know every mortal detail first. I was certain that she would exult in the whole bloody awful business, from what happened in Yonkers, to my physical struggle with Chadwin. I recoiled at the thought, and I was too confused to make explanations.

"I'm here for the knees-up!" she said, holding up the bottle of bourbon which Marty had taken with him when they departed.

Donna thought she smelled fun. Her senses weren't acute

enough to detect distress. She raised her eyebrows at Rovnik who retreated, unintroduced, to the lounge.

"You said you were going back..." I began gruffly.

"I said – you said – we say all sorts of foolish things, sweetie," Donna said, following me into the kitchen. "I see you like the older man."

"It's not like that, Donna. Mr Rovnik works for the County in this area..."

"I'll betcha he does! It makes the local taxes a little more bearable!" Donna came out with her grating laugh, as she poured her own bourbon, and submerged it in orange juice.

I took her through to the living room. I sensed that Donna would play up to him, so I said, "Mr Rovnik's taking me into Clayburg immediately. He's the County rat-catcher. We're going right now."

"Something wrong with your car, honey? I'll take you."

"Mr Rovnik's taking me, *now.*"

"Uh-huh. Just you and Mr Rovnik."

"Just finishin' my drink," Rovnik said. "Call me Earl."

"Why don't you slip into something loose, sweetie. You look as though you just finished the laundry," Donna said, as I went out of the door.

Rovnik and Donna bellowed with amusement.

I feared that Chadwin would escape at any moment, and that everything would unravel in front of Donna and Rovnik. I remembered the garage doors. I went to the electricity panel in the hall to find the isolation switch for them. That would mean they couldn't be opened; they were too stout to force. Chadwin would have to break through at the top of the stairs, or get out on the lakeside. I was confronted by a board with a mass of fuses and switches, mostly unmarked. In the few seconds I had, I couldn't work out which related to the garage doors. I slammed the panel shut without result, and ran back to the kitchen. I stood listening. Nothing from downstairs. Maybe Chadwin was having difficulty with my knots.

I halted outside the lounge door. Donna had switched on the hi fi. She had Rovnik on his feet, dancing. The pair swayed to the sugary big band music from one of our old CDs. Rovnik must have thought he was on the winner of all time with two randy women. He had his leather jacket off. He was a hard, tanned, muscular man despite his age. Donna had slipped off her anorak, and was pressing herself against Rovnik's chest. I didn't know how to break this up, but I knew that every moment which elapsed before I reported what had happened to the police, was a mark against me. And Chadwin could appear on the scene at any second.

A movement on the floor in the hall caught my eye, a slithering shadow. I moved to the kitchen door to get a better look. A rat was sitting preening itself in front of the clutter I had piled up against the workshop door. The creature had a scabby tail, and a white-haired snout with sores. I screamed.

Rovnik came blundering out of the living room, the dance music syruping on behind him.

"Whassa matter?" he asked, hitching his trousers and doing up his shirt buttons.

"It's a rat! Kill it, for God's sake."

"Where?" Rovnik asked, searching the bare boards of the hall.

"It was here a second ago. It must have got up here from the workshop."

"You sure?" Rovnik said, looking at me as though I was seeing things.

Donna came out of the living room, flushed and annoyed, smoothing her sweater and skirt.

"What's all the noise, honey? You jealous or something?"

"There's a horrible rat in the house!"

"Oh, darling. You are in a bad way. What you need is a couple more drinks, and a dance with Earl. There's plenty of him to go round," Donna said, her face smeared with lipstick and eye-shadow.

Rovnik was rolling his eyes at Donna, sending the silent message was that I was loopy. I lost myself momentarily.

"I must go now, please, please please! I said, my voice trembling and breaking.

I retreated to the kitchen, slamming the door closed. I was sobbing on the edge of hysteria. What I had to do, was to demand categorically that Rovnik take me to the police *now.* I hadn't mentioned the police to Donna. How could I get this log of a man moving? Suppose I switched to Donna? Got her to take me. She had offered. No, that course was impossible.

My confused thoughts were interrupted by the sound of an engine outside the window. I looked out. Rovnik was at the wheel of the yellow van, and moving slowly away. And a few seconds later, Donna's car pulled onto the road, tight behind the van. The two vehicles disappeared down the pine fringed road. Donna and Rovnik were going places together! I couldn't believe that they had left me without a word. I was alone with Chadwin again.

12

I had only two options now to avoid Chadwin. I could run down the road – it was at least three or four miles to the nearest cabin, which would probably be unoccupied; or try to extricate the Jeep from the garage. I had locked the workshop doors and it would take time for Chadwin to get through them. He would have plenty of implements to help him, but there was no noise which suggested a door being forced. I decided to take the chance that Chadwin had not yet forced his way out of the workshop.

I took the keys, let myself quietly out of the front door, and went down to the garage. The garage doors were closed. Inside the garage was quiet. I could not retreat now. I touched the remote to make room for the Jeep to be backed out. I slid into the driving seat, fumbling in the shadows, trying to get the key in the ignition. Then the key slid in, and at the first twist, the engine fired, and started with a roar like an aircraft. I shot the car backwards so violently, that I had to stamp on the brake to avoid running off the concrete forecourt, and into the ditch. The engine stalled. I was confronted by a dashboard of red lights. I twisted the ignition key frantically. Each time the engine fired, and died, fired, and died.

I leaped out of the vehicle and ran back toward the front door. As I mounted the steps, a moan of rage echoed down the hall. Chadwin burst through the barrier at the top of the workshop stairs. He appeared in his bloody shirt and underpants, his feet bare. He saw me. I backed down the front steps and ran around the corner of the house. I could hear Chadwin mouthing wild threats behind me. I wasn't thinking clearly of a route for myself. I didn't want to get into a chase along the road, or through the pines – which I would inevitably lose. I ran along the strip of lawn beside the house, and clambered over the trellis at the end. I was now on the lake side of the house.

The way along the front of the house, with the lounge patio above, was narrow and stony. The rock outcrop, on which the property was built, fell steeply to the water. The lakeside itself deepened suddenly, and was boulder-strewn. I started across the uneven ground, trying to pick my way as fast as I could. My knees and shins were painfully bruised. My legs moved with electric shocks of pain, as I gashed them on the stones, but there was no question of stopping.

I looked round to see Chadwin, raw and half-naked, calling inarticulately in the wind, struggling over the trellis behind me. On one side, I had the wall of the house. On the other, a boulder strewn drop to deep water. Ahead, I had an impossibly uneven path which could break my ankles. The only clear track was to the jetty.

The jetty extended thirty yards out onto the lake. After about thirty-five feet of thick wooden piles, it was a floating structure which tossed, and snaked on its pontoons in the rough water. Chadwin would catch me either on the rocks, or on the jetty. The end of the jetty was a treacherous place, where the water was fifteen feet deep. The movement of the lake to a nearby river outfall caused a rip current. Nobody ever swam from the jetty, even in high summer with clear water.

I feared Lake Chateaugay as well as loved it. At times, 'Pine Hill' seemed to me to be perched presumptuously near a dangerous beast. The lake claimed lives, summer after summer. It was moody, constantly changing its face in concert with the sky, the wind, and the forest. Serene translucence could turn to vicious cross currents in minutes. I had made this final mistake, instead of taking my chance on the road or in the forest. The jetty gave no hope; it gave only a short path to oblivion. I was committing myself to a force far more powerful than the one which was pressing me.

I stepped onto the moving boards, not sure that I could feel enough in my legs to keep balance. I passed the weathered sign that said, *Dangerous, Do Not Swim*. I went to the end, heaving up and down. I turned to face Chadwin, my hair flapping away from my head like a flag. My tracksuit was soaked by spray. I braced myself, legs apart. I had a last moment hope that Chadwin would see that however much he wanted to hurt me, the end of the jetty was not merely dangerous for both of us, but near suicidal. He was a predator with a vile and childish temper, but not, I still believed, a killer, or a suicide.

Chadwin advanced toward me along the boards. His thick shoulders swayed as he balanced. He crouched like a Sumo wrestler, his bull neck bent forward. His breath tore from his throat in cries. He had his arms out to grab me. He would thrash me, and drag me to the shore and rape me. He was demented, and oblivious of the danger. To him, the lake might have appeared as a piece of choppy water which held no fears for a capable swimmer. To me it was a cunning and deceptive wild animal.

We grappled. He took my feeble blows on his face and shoulders without effect, and dug his fingers deep into my upper arms, pinioning them. We fell on the soaking deck, which heaved itself up in a sudden wave, bigger than the rest. The deck dropped heavily after the swell, lurching sideways. We were tipped over the edge of the pontoon, down into the dark turbulence, clasped together.

Chadwin did not mean to let go of me! I choked and struggled, gulped the brackish water. Only when a more ruthless arm, the current, dragged us down, did he release me to save himself. The tide was peaty brown, clouded with silt from mountain streams. It was brutally cold. I kicked off my slippers, and flailed upward with all the remaining strength in my arms and legs. I could see the surface far above, like a sepia pane of rough glass. At the same time, I fought in the direction of the shallows near the shore. The cold had taken such possession of me, that I hardly felt my frozen skin, or any hurt from my bursting lungs.

13

Half conscious, I dragged myself into a shallow space between the rocks, under the shadow of our patio, and rested against a slab of granite.

As soon as I had the strength to walk, I waded out of the water, and on to the foot of the jetty. I looked along the lakeshore on either side to see a sign of Chadwin. A couple of times I started, mistaking a partly submerged log for a body, but that was all.

The climb to the house was like a mountainside, and I managed it very slowly. I got a pair of shoes, and a blanket which I wrapped around my wet clothes. I tried to start the Jeep. I churned the engine until the battery was flat. I couldn't remember where I had put the keys of Chadwin's car, and I didn't want to dally at the house. I walked along the road. Chadwin was either recovering, waiting to come after me, or drowned. Either way I needed urgent help.

It seemed to take hours to walk to the nearest cabin, but it was locked and deserted. I had walked perhaps another mile, when a car towing a boat stopped for me. The driver was friendly. With his help, I got to a phone, called the police who said they would alert the rescue services. And I managed to get Greg in Baltimore. He offered to get a flight to Rochester immediately. He was upset that he was too far away to be able to help, but I reassured him that the worst was over, and I could manage. My rescuer kindly turned his car around, and took me the ten or so miles back to 'Pine Hill', to wait for the police and emergency rescue services. I asked him to wait with me, and he did, for the best part of an hour, and then feeling safer, I urged him to go.

I stood for a time on the patio, peering into the tossing waters, until my head ached from the shafts of reflected light. Chateaugay was revelling in its strength. I have to admit that I was secretly, in my innermost heart, numb about Chadwin's death – if he was dead. The situation between us had become so monstrous that there didn't seem to be room for us both in life. But at the same time, gnawing at me, was the real possibility that a fit man like Chadwin might well have shrugged off his head injuries, and been swept along by the tide, but still managed to drag himself into the shallows hundreds of yards along the shore. He could be out there now, recovering from the ordeal.

More at ease now that the police were on their way, I swept and washed the spare bedroom floor again, folded the bloodstained sheets on the bed, and sprayed the room with air-freshener to reduce the odour of alchohol – there was no getting rid of it. The sheets stank. Then I washed all the glasses, poured out the remains of the bourbon left from the Kutash invasion, and put the bottles in the trash.

The County Lake Rescue Service were the first to arrive, in a truck, towing a rubber outboard boat, with four men, lines, nets, submersible torches, and frogman suits with scuba gear. I told the chief that a man went into the water from the end of the jetty over an hour ago.

"He fall in, lady?"

"Yes."

"Swimmer?"

"I don't know. I expect so."

"You look as though you've been in."

"I have."

"To save him?"

"He dragged me in. He attacked me on the jetty and it was so rough, we both fell in. I'll be making a full statement to the police. I've called them."

The chief looked piercingly at me as though what I said was contestable. "Sure is a dangerous place."

He asked if I was sure about the time it happened, thinking I suppose that a careful look along the shore or shallows might be more productive. But the team began their work in the deep, at the end of the jetty, with safety ropes, while I watched from the lounge room windows, my mind blocked.

The police arrived in a black car half an hour later, and I went down to it.

"I'm Detective Sergeant Gary Beckman, and this is Lieutenant Cavallo," the driver said.

"Thank goodness you've come," I said, actually feeling fearful and intimidated.

Cavallo had a pale face, with oily slicked back hair. He was thin and intense, and he looked tired. He and Beckman followed me upstairs. After watching the rescue services team out of the dining room window for a few moments, Cavallo turned to me.

"What happened, Mrs Stamford?"

"Like I said when I called, a man went into the lake, but that's…"

"What does *went in* mean Mrs Stamford?"

"We were struggling, the jetty was pitching, and we fell off."

"You look as though you've had a rough time."

"I have, I got all this," I said as I pulled my old sweater up to show him the bruising on my chest and side. "I've been assaulted, and subjected to…"

"We'll get you examined," Cavallo said carefully, seeming to anticipate criminal activity in the shadows around the few facts that were known to him. "Do you want to change your clothes?"

"No. I want to go home."

"We need to examine your clothes."

I tried to prepare myself for the awful questioning. I sat with the blanket around my shoulders, and my head pounding. Cavallo sent Beckman outside to talk to the Rescue Service, took a chair, and pointed to one for me. He put a small tape-recorder on the coffee table. He also slipped a shorthand notebook out of the side pocket of his creased grey suit, and flicked over the pages to find a space. A pen appeared in his hand, and he moved in the chair to accommodate his awkward left-handed style. "Tell me…"

I explained that I had arrived at the house that morning to clean up, and organise a sale. Dwight Chadwin arrived uninvited. He threatened me with rape. Forced me to the bedroom. We fought on the bed. I broke free, and knocked him unconscious with a baseball bat. I tied him up to safeguard myself, intending to call the police, but before I could, he got free. He chased me onto the jetty, we fought, and both fell into the water. I managed to save myself.

"Remarkable story, Mrs Stamford," Cavallo said, with a cynicism which I hoped he tagged to every statement he heard, rather than reserved for mine.

"It's true."

"Why did you run onto the jetty if you were afraid of being raped?"

"Because there was nowhere else to run!"

"Do you know Chadwin?"

"I met him at my club, and he came on to me."

"You didn't encourage him?"

"I'm a happily married woman."

"So he just appeared here, like that?"

"Yes. He must have followed me."

"Uh-huh," Cavallo said, pausing and staring at me with his button-bead eyes.

"Is this going to take long?" I asked.

"We can't go home because it's getting late, Mrs Stamford. We have to complete the first stage of our enquiry here, tonight. We need photos, measurements, statements."

Cavallo and Beckman moved cautiously around the house, inspecting. I sat mute in a corner of the lounge room. A carload of forensic technicians appeared, and after a short conference with Cavallo, changed into white overalls, and swarmed through the rooms with their brushes and plastic bags. The remains of the barrier was still partly blocking the workshop stairs. They removed this and went down, and through to the garage. Cavallo asked me to hand over my clothes. A woman technician came with me into the bedroom. She took everything I was wearing and dropped them into a plastic bag.

"Your chest must be painful," she said, sympathetically. "And when you're examined, don't forget to show this."

She pointed to bruises from Chadwin's fingers around my groin.

I went back to the lounge in another old tracksuit. I couldn't settle to take a shower. Cavallo soon came back to where I was sitting. "Those cars..."

After I had explained that the Jaguar was Chadwin's, Cavallo said, "It's parked in the garage, Mrs Stamford. Would a stalker park his car in your garage?"

"I'm pretty sure I left the doors open, and he must have driven in."

"The doors behind the Jaguar are closed, would a stalker do that?"

"He did."

"Quite a nerve. Sure of himself," Cavallo said, sceptically. "Another small point. How come the whiskey in the bedroom? Rapists don't generally settle down with a bottle of whiskey, and their victim."

I didn't know how to play this. I didn't reply.

"Detective Beckman tells me the bedclothes smell of whiskey, Mrs Stamford."

"Chadwin was drinking."

"You didn't join him in a drink?"

"No."

I was trying to keep the story basically true, but as simple as possible. I had to gloss over points which seemed unimportant, or change the facts slightly. I always had the Westchester court in my mind, and how what *really* happened there was changed by mentioning some facts and leaving out others, to fit the picture Chadwin and Shultz wanted to portray. Small, virtually irrelevant facts could be held against me – like having a drink with Chadwin in the bedroom.

Cavallo drove me to Clayburg to be examined by a doctor, and my bruises photographed. I could feel his silent displeasure pressuring me all the way. After the examination, he arranged for a police driver to take me back to Cedar Falls – I wasn't fit to drive.

"Mrs Stamford," he said, as I climbed into the police cruiser outside the doctor's surgery. "With all due respect to you, this is a homicide case, unless this man has managed to get to shore. There's a whole lot of things we don't know. Things that don't add up. We need your cooperation, and I don't think we've had it so far. Think about it!"

I felt like a stranger as I walked up to the door of our Cedar Falls home, past the neatly trimmed lawns, seeing signs of family habitation. Greg must have left Baltimore immediately after my call. He and the twins were back. A bike was collapsed in a hedge. A basketball rested in the rose garden, a baseball cap on the front steps. A window was open, a curtain blowing in the breeze, bringing sounds of young voices. A family lived in this house, and a woman was entering it, after being questioned by the police about what they suspected might be a murder; a woman who had kept part of her life in a secret compartment for years. And the secret compartment was leaking, like a broken sewer pipe, oozing a smelly mess over other lives in the family.

I let myself in. The stereo was blasting. Nobody was in the living room, dining room or kitchen. I went through to the games room at the back. I was deluged with tearful cuddles from the girls, with Greg and Grace waiting patiently behind.

"I've told them there's been an accident at the lake, and a man got drowned," Greg said.

"If he did," I replied.

"Do you seriously think Chadwin could have saved himself?"

"Why not? I did."

The children reverted to a serious, staring-eyed silence very quickly. Greg asked them to go to bed, and took my arm solicitously. He led me into the lounge. Grace followed.

"It's Chadwin isn't it?" she asked.

"Everything is all right, dear. It's all over now," Greg said.

"He attacked you again," Grace said.

It was fairly obvious from the look of me. "Yes he did, but he won't do it again," I said.

"How do you know?"

"Because the police will get him."

"But the other man…"

"Schultz is dead."

"You know that?"

"I do. We're both safe."

Grace sobbed. Greg put his arm round her shoulders. "You go up and see the children are in bed, and go to bed yourself. There's nothing to cry about."

As she went hesitantly out of the door, Grace looked back, and her beautiful, panic-stricken face made me want to cry. Grace didn't believe us. And I didn't believe entirely, either. Chadwin was indestructible. He had qualities which were not human or civilised. He was smashing my life – the life of our family – like a demolition ball.

"You look all in," Greg said to me when she had gone. "Do you want a rest? We can talk later."

"I don't feel well, Greg. I'll use the spare room in case I disturb you."

Greg looked slightly disappointed. He was trying to encourage me, and I was withdrawing. I couldn't help it. I wanted to be away from everybody.

I went upstairs and pulled back the covers in the spare bedroom. I kept the bed made up and aired for the babysitter. I knew what I was going to do, and I felt numb, utterly weak. I had in mind the Zen saying *Just do it!* I was going to do it by the simplest route. No preparations, no anticipation, no more thinking. I peeled off my tracksuit, and kicked off my trainers. I stank. I hadn't had a shower since I plunged into the lake. My hair hung in sticky threads, my fingernails were broken, my hands grimed, my teeth were slimy, my mouth tasted of blood and ash and the rank taste of river water.

I went into the ensuite bathroom in our bedroom, and opened the cabinet. In a transparent jar, set behind the bottles of bath foam and moisturiser, were sleeping pills. It was always the same, that jar, because Greg and I seldom used the pills. I emptied three pills from the jar on to my palm, and washed them down with a glass of water. A pale, mussed, blond woman, with grey smears on her face, looked at me from the mirror; her dead eyes were like raw oysters on the shell. A stranger.

"Just do it," I whispered, and spread a handful of pills on my palm this time.

I was completely worn down. The two possibilities confronting me seemed like vast boulders, impacting to crush the life out of me – face Chadwin again in the street, or face a murder enquiry, and all the disgusting sludge that would leak out as it progressed.

I filled the glass with water. When I looked up, Greg was in the mirror. He was standing behind me, watching. He stepped forward, took my wrist firmly, and shook the pills into the hand-basin.

"How many have you taken?"

I was silent for a few moments, and then I said, "Only a couple."

Greg squinted at the level in the jar, and seemed satisfied.

"I'll take care of these," he said, removing the jar, and turning me round gently.

"You've been through it," he started softly, "but don't take that cowardly way out. People here need you. I do. The children. And Grace. You did your best to deal with Chadwin when he surfaced again in your life. Don't hold yourself responsible. You're just a leaf in the stream…"

I looked up at him, rested my fingers on his cheek. "Thanks, Greg."

"Loren, talk to me…"

"I want to rest, please, Greg."

"Aren't you going to shower?"

"I'm just going to bed," I said, and I went into the spare bedroom, closed the door and crawled, naked and dirty, between the crisp sheets. As soon as my head touched the pillow, I was falling, plunging down into complete darkness.

My head was full of disturbing shapes and noises, which at first seemed meaningful, but I found eventually, after a struggle to understand, had no meaning, and filled me with a deep sense that I could not achieve whatever it was I was seeking. The surreal futility of the dream woke me.

The curtain by the open window was moving in the draught. It was dark outside, the neighbourhood silent. I looked around the deeply shadowed room. It was like being in a friend's house, known, but still strange. I'd never slept in this room before. By the wardrobe was a deeper shadow, and the way the light fell around this area made it look as though somebody was standing there. I dismissed the thought, and let my eyes travel on round the room, past the dressing table, the bureau, the cheval mirror, the big lampshades, the heavy drapes, and outside – I had left the drapes open – in the moonlight, a blurred view of treetops and a neighbour's roof.

My eyes returned to the deep shadow by the wardrobe. Was there a movement there, somebody standing quietly, watching? It was Greg, my poor worried husband… No, Greg had no need to watch from a secret place. The only person it could be was Chadwin! Chadwin risen from the tide of the river.

I dispelled the thought. Imagination. Unreasonable fear. Surely, the first thing Chadwin would do, if he saved himself, and he could not lay hands on me, would be to go to his wife. How could I see him in my bedroom in the middle of the night? He was a marketing director, not a cat burglar. I was becoming more accustomed to the half darkness. I could make out objects like a silver photo-frame on the dressing table, and my discarded sweater over a chair. It *was* somebody! The shadow came to life. Chadwin!

The wide-shouldered and thick-necked figure that stepped towards me could not be mistaken. I could see a crumpled open shirt, the beefy forearms, the hands that had locked my arms as we went down in the lake. He had a pair of trousers on now.

The scream was inside me, bursting my head, but not coming out, because I was being taken too quickly. Chadwin bounded across the room, and crushed an open palm across my mouth, shoved me back into the pillow, mashing my nose and lips.

"I'm going to finish the job, bitch!" he hissed.

He tore the sheet away, and threw himself on top of me, spreading my legs, pinning my arms, and raising an arm over me. I could see the broken bottle in his hand, jagged at the neck. I writhed under his weight, but it was like trying to move a huge stone, a stone that smelled of river damp and rotting logs. I twisted, and tried to turn, but my strength had leaked away like the yolk from a broken egg. Chadwin levered himself off me and plunged the bottle. I screamed. I could feel it tearing, searing, lacerating me from groin to navel.

14

Suddenly the room was flooded with light. There was perfect silence.

"What the devil's going on?" Greg said quietly, standing at the foot of the bed in his pyjamas.

I was flat on my back on the mattress, the bedclothes and pillows on the floor. I was wet. My body ached. My breasts felt bruised, even my mouth and nose where Chadwin had crushed them. My groin was on fire. But there was no Chadwin.

"A bad dream, huh?" Greg said, sitting beside me on the bed, and reaching out to touch me reassuringly.

A small face peeped around the door with an enquiring look.

"You OK, Mom?" Rosemary asked.

I said I had a bad dream, and Greg got up to take the child back to bed.

"Gosh, those are awful marks, Mom," Rosemary said as she was being carried out of the door.

When he came back, Greg said I was making enough noise to wake the neighbours, let alone the kids.

"It was Chadwin, trying to kill me."

"The chances are he's dead, Loren."

I didn't say any more. I drew Greg down beside me, and felt the peace of him flowing into me. After a few minutes, I rose, had a shower, washed my hair, and made two chocolate malts; then we curled up to sleep in our own bedroom. I slept dreamlessly.

The next day, I called in sick at Ulex. Greg phoned me from the office telling me that the local TV and radio had a mysterious missing-person-in-the-lake story. "Something cobbled up from police reports."

Cavallo was on the doorstep by mid-afternoon. I invited him inside and made him a cup of coffee.

"Nice home you have here, Mrs Stamford," he said ruminatively as he sipped the coffee, and looked around at the furnishings.

In my over-sensitive state, I thought that he was implying that the home might be in jeopardy, and it rattled me.

"I think it's about time you told us what actually happened at the lake. Mr Rovnik a county officer has come forward. And we've also spoken to a Mrs Kutash whom he named."

I sat quietly for a while, and so did Cavallo. He had dark smears under his eyes which made him look sinister, although his manner was easy. He had a capacity for quiet which didn't seem to fit a police lieutenant. I had wanted to keep Rovnik and Donna Kutash out of it, because they would only cloud the case, but that was impossible now.

"You didn't mention Mr Rovnik or Mrs Kutash," Cavallo said reproachfully.

"Why? They had nothing to do with it."

"Were they there when Chadwin was there?"

"No. Before."

"Mr Rovnik said you first spoke to him a couple of weeks ago when he was working at the lake."

"That's true. I was worried about the rats."

"He says that on another occasion you used him to get rid of an unwelcome caller."

"True. That was Donna Kutash's husband who was making a nuisance of himself."

"And on the day of the alleged drowning, you invited him inside, gave him a drink, and told him you had a man in the house who was threatening you. The part about a man in the house wasn't true, because you've already told me Chadwin wasn't there."

"That's right. It was Mr Kutash."

"In the house?"

"Well, I thought he might arrive."

"Mrs Stamford, Mr Rovnik says he thought you were interested in him. And it kinda looks that way."

"That's absolutely wrong. I felt insecure. I wanted protection."

"Mr Rovnik says you made a fuss about seeing a rat in the hall."

"I did."

"He thought you were acting jealously, because he was paying attention to Mrs Kutash."

"There was a rat, and I was revolted by it. I had no interest in Mr Rovnik."

"Why did you invite him inside the house?"

"I wanted to persuade him to take me to Clayburg immediately. That's the only reason."

"Why go to Clayburg?"

"To get to a phone to call the police and my husband."

"But no wrong had been committed against you."

"I felt threatened."

"Mrs Kutash says she called in to your place around one pm. She was in the kitchen and the front room. She passed through the hall. There was broken glass, an ice-bucket, and bloodstained rags on the floor, in an alcove in the hall."

"I was cleaning up the house."

"Mrs Kutash says she thought you had a man there, and were trying to get rid of her."

"Donna Kutash is a dirty minded bitch!" I said, stung. "I love my husband. I don't have other men."

Cavallo paused, his eyelids moving slowly as he blinked, whether out of tiredness or exasperation.

"We found the remains of two crystal glasses, and a bottle of bourbon in the trash. Who were you drinking with, Mrs Stamford?"

"Nobody. I threw away a cracked glass, that's all. The other was used by Chadwin."

"The fragments of both glasses and the bottle have signs of blood on them."

"Probably contaminated in the trash."

"You have some ready answers, Mrs Stamford. We'll want to check whose blood that is."

"Sure."

"The medical report on you says you have cuts on your feet and one arm – apart from bruising. Mr Rovnik says your arm was bleeding when he met you at the door of your place around the middle of the day."

"I cut it in the workshop."

"We've found a pair of jeans and a sweater and underwear, newly washed in the washing machine."

"I changed my clothes."

"We think there are traces of bloodstains on them."

"I changed after Chadwin beat me up."

"Mr Rovnik says you were wearing a green track-suit – the one you handed to us – when you invited him inside."

"He's mistaken."

"If he's right, Chadwin was already at your house, and the assault had happened."

"I don't know ...I'm all mixed up."

I had made a lot of facile answers. Being interrogated was like trying to cross a fast-flowing stream. Each answer was a stepping stone, and I felt momentarily safe – but then I had to find another stepping stone, and another, always in danger of falling. Cavallo wasn't drawing any conclusions in front of me about my stumbling performance.

He rose to go, and said mournfully, "I'll be back. I don't have to tell you Mrs Stamford that there are serious penalties for obstructing a police investigation."

Later in the afternoon, Donna Kutash called me.

"Wow! Darling, have you been having a ball!"

"Donna, I haven't."

"Bucky is missing. In the lake! Jesus, Loren, what happened?"

"I don't know," I said helplessly.

"What kind of tricks were you guys up to? I mean, I *knew* Bucky was there, and you two were – you know?"

"Nothing. You've got it completely wrong."

"I had the police here, Loren. *The police!*"

"I know."

"I didn't realise you were in some kind of trouble. I thought..."

"I don't want to talk about it."

"Well, hell, darling, I can help you."

"Just tell the police what you know, and lay off all your assumptions."

"What do you want me to tell them, Loren? Anything you tell me, I tell them. Gospel."

"You've already spoken to them."

"Oh, yeah. But I was none too sure, and I can remember better for the police if you tell me what happened."

"No, Donna."

"I'm trying to help you, honey."

"No."

"I'm your friend."

"I know."

"Wow! Bucky Chadwin. He was one nice guy. And what a looker."

Donna was peeved. Her tone changed. "Eve Chadwin is pretty pissed. I spoke to her. I mean… her husband in the lake. He is in the lake isn't he, Loren?"

"I told you I can't talk about it."

"Well, dear, you really are a one," Donna said, ringing off abruptly.

Cavallo telephoned me a few days later to say that the County Lake Rescue Service had recovered Chadwin's body. I said no more than "Yes", but privately I flooded with relief, and a very slight sense of triumph. The man had got what he deserved. He would haunt me no longer. And I felt no guilt for his death. Apart from submitting to Chadwin's will, I believed I could not have done anything other than I did to save myself.

The local news media gave a lot of space to the violent death, particularly because Chadwin was a senior executive with a local company. Greg and I, identified as the owners of the property where it happened, were under a cloud. We could do no more than refuse to speak to the reporters who door-stepped, and photographed us.

A few days later, Cavallo telephoned again, saying that the County pathologist had reported that Chadwin died from drowning, although he had heavy cranial bruising, which could have caused unconsciousness, before immersion. The pathologist was clear that these injuries could not have been received in the tide. Cavallo's tone underlined this finding heavily.

"Chadwin also had lacerations to his hands, knees and the soles of his feet, caused before immersion, which were inflicted by broken glass; fragments of glass were found in his feet," Cavallo said. "Do you want to comment on this?"

"No."

He made a date, a day later, to come to the house. "More questions, Mrs Stamford," he said, ominously.

I had some misgivings about the meeting, but I told Greg, who offered to be present, that I could deal with it alone. When Cavallo called at the house, I was still on sick leave. He had Beckman with him. He seemed relaxed, more smartly dressed, and on top of his task. He refused the offer of coffee, and stood in the hall, with Beckman. I sensed, then, that this was a formal moment, a bad moment for me.

"Mrs Stamford, I'm going to caution you on suspicion of being involved in the murder of Dwight Chadwin. Anything you say may be used in evidence against you, and you're entitled to have a lawyer present."

Beckman waved a small tape recorder, and gave a much more wordy version of the caution, asking me if I understood.

"I understand. I'm prepared to talk, if you wish," I said, hoping – vainly, I suppose – that I could bail myself out.

I could see that these two men were at the point in their work where they got an adrenalin rush. They were alert, slightly flushed. They watched me like two wolves ready to attack and feed.

"We know that the latest fingerprints on the steering wheel of Chadwin's Jaguar car are yours. Whether you travelled in the car with Chadwin or alone, *you* parked it in the garage. Why would you drive and park a stalker's car?"

"OK, I parked it. I wanted it out of the way until the police came, because I didn't want to have to explain to anybody why it was there."

"Who is anybody?"

"Any nosy people like the Kutashs."

"Mrs Kutash remembers seeing the car keys in the lake house, and asking you about them."

"I told you she was nosy."

"But if this terrible assault on you was going on, why not tell, and get help?"

"I wanted the police, not her."

"But why, when Mrs Kutash's presence could protect you?"

"Because Chadwin was an acquaintance of hers. She'd have insisted on his release, and he would have got away with his assault on me."

Cavallo paused to consider this, and then changed the subject.

"So Chadwin's keys were, as Mrs Kutash says, in the house, and that means Chadwin was in the house?"

"Yes."

"And you lied about this ...why?"

"I didn't want Kutash – or Rovnik – in my face. I wanted the police."

"In fact, what Mrs Kutash saw, the broken glass in the hall, means that a violent scene had already taken place between you and Chadwin?"

"Yes, apart from what happened on the jetty."

"You could have put Chadwin's unconscious body on a sheet, dragged it down the path to the jetty, and pushed it into the water, couldn't you?"

"I doubt I'd have been strong enough. I've told you the truth about that. He chased me on to the jetty!"

"Mrs Stamford, we have two different blood groups on the broken glass. One is Chadwin's, and we believe the other is yours. The fact is, you were drinking with Chadwin before his death."

The Westchester spectre of drink was materialising again. "I never killed him!"

15

Greg and I decided that we would stick to our plan to leave our jobs, and leave Cedar Hills, despite the fact that Chadwin himself was now no longer a threat. The anxieties generated around his death had a lot to do with that decision. The possibility that I would be prosecuted for murder seemed to be increased by newspaper publicity, at least in my mind. The first newspaper and TV reports linked the possible drowning with me. There were only two characters in the drama – Chadwin and me. A man missing, presumed drowned, at a lonely lakeside house occupied by me. These were suspicious circumstances, made all the more interesting by Chadwin's wealthy and distinguished family. The obvious inference was that we were having an affair.

When the facts moved on to the discovery of a drowned man, who had probably been beaten unconscious before drowning, the spectre of murder hovered over every report.
And this was boosted by the revelation, only a matter of a couple of days after my written statement to Cavallo, of the Westchester Court story. A stooge in the police department leaked it. Jed Willard my lawyer was philosophical about this development.

"It's too good a story to wind up in police records, Loren," he said, "and some bum has sold it to the press for a few bucks."

A local tragedy with sexual overtones was propelled into a state-wide cause celebre. *Sex Attacker Haunts Victim*, *Fatal Meeting Between Victim and Attacker* were the style of lurid headlines. A repellent patina of glamour was added, and guaranteed wide coverage, because the Chadwin family were politically connected in New York State. Eve Chadwin's family had similar distinctions. Even Grace's mental illness, and Duane Schultz's violent death were used to add titillation.

It was a time when I felt I couldn't hold my head up in the face of people's stares, and I was tempted to get my doctor to give me a medical certificate to say I was suffering from stress, and couldn't attend the office. But I didn't. I went to work.

After the papers and media had been burning for a week, the human resources boss at Ulex hauled me into her office. Jane Dodds was effusive in a sickly way.

"I know you're going through a difficult time, Loren. Would you like to stand down for a time? I've spoken with Jack Driscoll and it's okay by him. Paid leave, of course," she smarmed, like a children's nurse doling out candy.

It made me mad. I was an embarrassment at Ulex. They wanted me out of sight. I knew all the tricks. They'd block me coming back for a time, and then say they were reorganising and I was redundant. I'd be well paid, but effectively fired.

"No, I want to work, thanks."

"We're trying to be generous and sympathetic here, Loren."

"Well, that's very nice, Jane, but I want to work."

"Uh-huh," she said, considering I guess whether she could press me any further.

"That's fine," she said finally, "you just carry on."

The problem with the staff – as opposed to the narrow minded management – was an understandable one. They had a thirst to know the grisly details. I didn't socialise with any of them, or go to the canteen. I went only to the most necessary meetings. I worked hard in my office, and cleared my backlog. I faced looks that were partly compassionate, and partly uncomprehending. I felt as though I was inside an illuminated glass bubble. I was insulated from those around me, unable to communicate – what could I say? – and under searching examination.

Greg kept up my courage by saying that the media interest would wane after a few days, but neither of us spoke the unspeakable: that the media were constrained by the possibility that I might be charged with murder, and couldn't be tried publicly – yet.

Greg was chosen for the job in Buffalo, a genuine career move, and I thought the management of Ulex gave a collective sigh of relief when I gave notice, shortly after, that I was leaving. It was hard for them to pretend that nothing much had happened. I received a whole sheaf of sympathetic letters, and a lot of hugs, from colleagues. Whether I was going to be tried or not, I now had a vivid past which made me stand out beyond the quiet, relatively colourless finance executive that I should have been, was previously, and was expected to be. My background was an area of covert interest, and comment, and speculation, and my necessary contact with senior executives in other companies made my history more obtrusive. When the flush of publicity had gone, my past would still be there, sexually radiant, like a peacock's tail or a baboon's ass behind me. It would last as long as this generation of staff speculated about their bosses over the coffee machine in the corridor.

"That's Loren Stamford. A guy raped her when she was in her teens, and was found dead in the lake beside her house fifteen years later."

It was hardly necessary to say more. It was ugly. It was unfair, but it was a fact. The only possible way to mitigate this was by retreating.

The weeks while we tidied up our affairs for the move to Buffalo were therefore full of raw embarrassment and shame for me. The police investigation hung over my head. It was not personal shame about anything I had done, but the shame of being unfairly stigmatised by other people. Even the parents at

Mt. Vernon school, whom we met on car-runs, and at functions at the school, began to avoid me.

On a Saturday morning at seven-thirty, the telephone rang. We were in bed. The kids were charging around the house with Grace. Greg took the call.

"It's Sergeant Beckman," Greg said, handing the phone to me, flexing his jaw anxiously.

I felt the usual chill I had before these calls. I could hear the sounds from the police precinct at the other end, raucous voices, boots clumping on the floor, radio messages crackling. I was part of these machinations.

"Mrs Stamford?" Beckman said tonelessly, "I want to tell you that our advice from the DA's office, received yesterday, is that …" and here he hesitated cruelly.

"Can you hear me, Mrs Stamford?"

"Yes," I choked.

Greg had paled, and he put his arm around my shoulders.

"On the evidence we presently have, and I stress that Mrs Stamford, *on the evidence we presently have*, it is not proposed to bring any charges. You will have to give evidence at the inquest into the death."

"Thank you for telling me…" I replied, giving Greg a thumbs up sign.

Beckman's words brought an unbelievable glow of ease, words I had almost given up real hope of hearing.

"We'll need a further statement for the inquest."

"I'll let you know my new address."

I knew that Beckman and Cavallo really believed I murdered Chadwin, and they weren't going to let me forget it. They didn't seem to count what I'd been through. Murder was merely murder to them. They wanted the threat of a future murder trial to hang over me. That was as much punishment as they could give. But my heart was innocent, and I knew there could be no more evidence.

I put the phone down, and rolled over toward my husband. I put my arms round him, and kissed him. He pulled back my head, searching me.

"You know, Loren, all I've heard from you is jagged bits and pieces...I know what's in the statement that you made for Jed, but I don't know what you felt, and thought at the time..."

I made sure that Grace could occupy the children for another hour. Then I fetched two cups of coffee from the kitchen, and we settled ourselves with a couple of pillows, propped up against the bedhead. The whole story had been something I shied away from whenever I could. *Tell him everything. Just do it!* I said to myself.

"It all started about fifteen years ago," I said to Greg, taking his hand. "I was nineteen, living with Grace and my father in Tarrytown, Westchester County. It was a Saturday afternoon in June. Grace and I were out walking. We were on a street where there are a lot of factories, deserted on a Saturday. A car passed, a chromed up old red and white Chevrolet, with two guys in it. The car stopped. The guys wanted to pick us up. They didn't manhandle us into the car, but because there weren't any people around, they kidded some, and wouldn't take no for an answer. They kinda hustled us into the car, although we didn't really want to go. As I found out later, one of the guys was named Duane Schultz, and the other..."

Later in the morning, Jed Willard my lawyer, called me.

As soon as I heard his voice, I said, "Oh Jed, I was going to call you Monday morning. Thanks for giving me my life back!"

"Ah! You've heard. Great. The DA called me. I know him."

"What did he say? Beckman just gave me the message."

"Well... you're sure you want to hear?"

"After what I've been through, I'm armour-plated."

"He said he had two very experienced police officers who knew a murder when they saw it. He thought the state had cogent circumstantial evidence of first degree murder, but they didn't have a witness to contradict you. Kutash and Rovnik are bit players. He said that although you would be shown to be a liar, the jury would be understanding about a decent – and attractive – wife, and you would get the sympathy vote…"

"*Sympathy*, Jed? Aren't I worthy of belief? What about the facts? You're the one who was insistent about telling the whole truth."

"What I said about telling the truth, as you know it, goes one hundred percent, but when it comes to the hearing, there are few absolute facts, only conflicting stories about what happened, told by different people."

"Funny, that's more or less what the attorney at Westchester said, years ago. He said something like, 'No can do reality.' Well, Jed if it hadn't been for you…"

"Loren, an innocent person can't get any closer to a charge of premeditated murder than you have…"

16

My story is pretty much as I have told it – and as it appeared in my statement to the police. I say, pretty much. The inquest, which Jed Willard steered me through produced lurid publicity. For the first time, the public had the details of what happened, but at least it was an uncontradicted version of my story. And it led to a verdict of death by misadventure. I moved with Greg, the children and Grace to Buffalo, and we made a fresh start. We sold the Park Drive property, and 'Pine Hill' without any problems, and the new house was in a quiet area, and very comfortable. Greg was buoyant about his new opportunities. Grace had settled down after the agony. The children coped easily at their new school. I got a place in a bank (with a glowing reference from Excel, to give them credit), and in a couple of years, I expected my career as a finance executive would be back on track. I was, as Jed Willard said, very lucky to get away without being charged. I didn't think I would ever be indicted now, because there couldn't be any new evidence that could come forward. Everything happened between Chadwin and me. My word against his, and he wasn't here.

In the course of my story, I may have appeared to be a sap, more acted on than acting. But that isn't quite me. I'm more flinty than that. I know that this doesn't tally with the fact that I tried to commit suicide when I came back from 'Pine Hill'. Suicide seems like an act of complete weakness, and only somebody who knew *all* the facts (not Greg or Jed Willard or Lieutenant Cavallo) would be able to get that in proportion. Nobody knows all the facts except me, and I suppose Chadwin, but he doesn't count now. I'm tougher than I appear. Being brought up in Tarrytown, my experience with my father, the rape, and the Westchester court toughened me underneath in a way probably even Greg doesn't appreciate.

When I had had time to get over the shock of seeing Chadwin again, and realise that he was going to threaten everything I had worked for, and my little family, I couldn't let him get away with it. In my heart I determined I would fight. That wasn't a simple declaration I made to myself or to Greg. It was a deeply private decision, forged in white heat. It didn't mean I was going to stand up to Chadwin publicly; it did mean that I was going to use every wile and every nerve to beat him, and if in the extreme it came to a physical confrontation, yes, I planned to fight until I dropped – or Chadwin killed me. If events had moved at a slower pace, and as a family we were able to leave town as we planned, I guess this resolve would be abandoned, because our problem would be solved – but events didn't turn out that way.

I honestly did everything I could to swerve Chadwin aside, to persuade him not to pursue me, but I saw it was hopeless. He said, when he was at 'Pine Hill', that the police wouldn't take any notice of his assault, because I had invited him. Well, the truth is, I *did* invite him. This is one of those significant little facts which I omitted from my story, and would deny utterly and forever to Greg, Jed Willard and Lieutenant Cavallo. I cast Chadwin as a stalker in my story to the police, which he undoubtedly was, but he was not a stalker in going to 'Pine Hill'.

I realised when I was in Jed Willard's office on the first occasion that he wouldn't let me say one thing, and tell the police something different. So, as I spelled out this story to him, for my police statement, I had to decide whether there was anything I couldn't tell him. I heeded his warning not to get tangled in the legal mowing machine, but I heeded even more Attorney Bronstein's remark – which Willard echoed later – that there is no reality about a crime, only evidence of a past event. In this case, my incontestable story that I never invited Chadwin to 'Pine Hill'. And there were a few other events where I thought my evidence had to be preferred to 'reality'.

I planned to have a confrontation with Chadwin at 'Pine Hill' in which reason and decency would 'free' us both to go our separate ways, or we would clash with incalculable results. If we were to clash violently, I intended to win. I suppose that means I contemplated killing Chadwin – murder if necessary, but it wasn't an issue that came to the surface of my mind at the time as such. I chose the baseball bat as my weapon, and it was not in the hall alcove, but handy in a corner of the bedroom, behind a dresser (just a little deviation from reality). I also knew that if we got to the stage of violence, that it could only be approached by pretending to submit. I had to get Chadwin in an unguarded position. All that happened.

Of course I had no idea of the events which might occur to frustrate my plans. The appearance of the Kutashs and Rovnik at the wrong times led me into a quagmire of small lies, which heightened the likelihood that I would be prosecuted. Their intervention was very dangerous for me.

At the time Donna and Rovnik were dancing around the lounge at 'Pine Hill' and Chadwin was trying to free himself in the workshop, I genuinely intended to notify the police and hand him over. I thought that act would neuter him, and I was confident my story would prevail. But when Donna and Rovnik deserted me, and I was on my own, I sank into that cold-hearted hopelessness I had felt when I invited Chadwin to come to the house. Desperate, I grasped the baseball bat again, moved the barrier at the top of the stairs, and went down to the workshop. I was going for him, even if he killed me.

I found Chadwin struggling to free his arms. I told him all this was unnecessary if only he would abandon his hateful intentions. He responded with foul swear-words.

I had learned my sailor's knots well. When I tied his wrists behind his back, I did so using two separate cords. The first, placed immediately around his wrists, and involving five or six coils, had the knot placed as far up and away from his fingers as I could get it. The second cord was around the top of his forearms and elbows, and impossible to slide downwards because a loop ran around his throat. This was a trick I remembered from a crime thriller I had read years ago. Chadwin had to sever two cords to free himself, the second in an awkward position in the middle of his back.

Chadwin had already released the first pinion. He had used an empty wine-crate as a platform to climb on to the workbench, and dislodge a hack-saw from the panel of tools which hung on studs on the wall, above the bench. Working from behind his back, he had managed to clamp the hack-saw vertically in the vice, which was screwed to the bench. With the wine crate as a footing, he was able to back on to the blade of the hack-saw, and work his arms up and down sufficiently to cut the lower cords.

When he saw me, he bellowed, jumped down, and charged, intending to knock me over or head-butt me. But I had the space, the time and the will to swing the bat hard against him. My first blow hit his shoulder and he stopped momentarily. I swung again, and this time the bat connected with his ear. He fell on his knees; his head must have been made of iron. I hit him again on the top of his skull. At last he collapsed on the concrete floor, unconscious.

Here, I probably made a grave mistake. I thought I had killed him although I was too repulsed to examine him closely. He was inert, his mouth bleeding, hanging open. He didn't seem to be breathing. As I recovered my breath, I confess I felt like David must have felt about Goliath. Before apprehension and uncertainty set in, I was exultant.

At one point in the police enquiry, Lt Cavallo had said that I could have dragged Chadwin's body, on a sheet, to the jetty and dumped him in the water. When Cavallo said that, I had an eerie feeling that he was looking inside my head. What I had thought, in that moment in the workshop, was that I could load Chadwin's body on one of the low trolleys we use to move the sailboats from the workshop to the lakeside. I visualised what would happen. I could cut away what was left of Chadwin's bonds, and heft his bulk on to the chassis of the trolley inch by inch. I could open the workshop doors, and let the trolley gradually down the slope. The wind was fierce. Rain, and foam from the lake would be churning in the air. The solid part of the jetty would be easy to negotiate, but not the pontoon; it would writhe. I would have to get the trolley well out on this structure so that the tide would carry the body away. I could tip Chadwin and the trolley into the water. The trolley would sink, and the body would be carried away by the tide. Then I would go for help.

My mind seized up when my thoughts got this far. How could I explain how Chadwin got into the lake? I was so exhausted, I wasn't capable of reasoning beyond this mechanical task of getting Chadwin into the water.

I turned, ran upstairs, and went out to the garage to get the Jeep out, as I've told. What I didn't realise was that Chadwin was still very much alive, crazed, and that he would come after me. Chadwin chased me on to the jetty, as I've said, and filled in the reality of what happened in the lake.

I was unrepentant about my deviations from the truth because I considered that I was defending not just my body, but everything dear to me. With these few final facts the real story will remain my secret.

17

On an evening about three months after we had moved to Buffalo, Greg and I were both home from work. We had put the girls to bed. Grace was out at a flower arranging class. We were in the lounge together talking about a vacation we were planning in Europe. The telephone rang, and Greg took the call.

He listened for a moment, and then I saw a confused look come over his face.

"Look, my wife has been through a lot..." he said.

He listened again for a few seconds and became quite agitated. His arms and legs were twitching as though he wanted to spring to his feet and couldn't, and his face was reddening. I had a feeling like a cold stone in my stomach. Although I had no idea who the caller was, the reference to me meant that it had to be about Chadwin.

"I can't see any point or reason for this, and if you won't tell me..." Greg said to the caller, and then he covered the mouthpiece with his hand. "It's Eve Chadwin, for you. She won't say what she's calling about."

I was sickened by the thought of any connection with the Chadwins, but I had done with running, and I had gone beyond the fear of confrontations on the subject.

"I'll tell her you're just not going to talk to her or anybody else, that you've had it way up over your head, and if she won't speak to me, then the hell with her!"

"I'll talk, Greg."

Greg relented with a little nod of admiration. "You're very resilient, my dear."

I took the receiver. "Yes?"

Eve's tone was matter-of-fact. "I'd like to see you. I don't want to talk on the telephone."

"How long will this take and where?" I said, trying to project a level voice.

"Twenty minutes. Say the lobby of the Hilton."

"Why now, Mrs Chadwin?"

"That's part of it. Let's meet."

She wasn't pleading. She wasn't commanding. I paused. But of course I was going to see her. "I can make the Hilton by 1pm tomorrow."

"Fine," she said, ringing off.

Greg and I speculated about what could be behind her call, and in the end fixed ourselves a stiff nightcap and went to bed, mystified, and depressed. The leaden clouds of a possible indictment had cleared away since we had been in Buffalo, but now a small grey smudge had appeared on the horizon.

I worked at First Capital about two blocks away from the Buffalo Hilton, and I arrived there at a couple of minutes short of 1pm. I was sure Eve wasn't amongst the scattering of people standing around, or lounging in the lobby chairs. I waited by the doors. At a few minutes past the hour, Eve drew up, driving a powder blue Bentley convertible. She abandoned the car to a bell-man, and walked proudly inside. She was wrapped in a beige camel-hair coat, and had big diamond studs in her ears. To me, she looked attractive, brittle, and a little worn. I felt anxious, but hard.

"Let's sit down, as privately as we can," she said without expression when she saw me.

We steered through the furniture to a couch in a corner. We both perched on the edge of the couch, at each end, half facing each other. Eve had an ugly designer handbag, with belts and buckles on it, which she placed in the space between us. She reached inside and pulled out a black box, which she pushed along the seat towards me.

"It's a tape-recorder. Switch it on, and listen. Hold it to your ear if you like. Go on."

She showed no particular emotion. I picked up the instrument, and started it. I heard my own voice.

'This is no good. We have to talk.'

'Sure we can talk honey, but where? This half-baked stuff at the club doesn't work. We need to get together,' Chadwin laughed.

'The only reason I want to see you is to reach an understanding,' I said.

'Oh, yeah, I want you to understand me, honey.'

'I'll be up at 'Pine Hills' on Lake Chateaugay next Saturday.'

'Hey, that's a nice idea. Marty told me about the lake. I've been meaning to look it over. He has a place up there.'

'You'll come up?'

'Will I what? You've got it, kid.'

'Late morning.'

'OK.'

As I lowered the tape-recorder, Eve pushed a small diary across the space between us.

"Take a look at that. It's my husband's private diary."

I opened the diary at the marked page. The entry for the date Chadwin visited 'Pine Hill' was, *am: LS, Chateaugay* in neat handwriting.

"So my husband never stalked you to Chateaugay," Eve said, "contrary to your account to the police."

"You only have to listen to that tape to understand what he was like..." I said, unable to refute her, and trying to order my thoughts.

Eve gave a short, dry laugh. "I know what he was like."

"You didn't hand this material to the police..."

What confused me most of all was that I couldn't understand Eve. Was she trying to torture me before she told the police? After all, although our physical contact had been slight, I was the woman in a revolting story that had upset her life. Eve's manner was oddly detached. There seemed to be nothing vengeful in her attitude toward me.

"I've only known about the tape and the diary for a few weeks," she said. "The tape is from Bucky's private line at the office. He always recorded his stuff, and kept it for a while. The tape was one of a number that came to me with his belongings, including the diary, from Hudson. I don't know why I played the tapes. It wasn't sentiment. Curiosity about this man who had left a space in my life. The diary – I'd never seen it before – he must have kept at the office for private commitments."

"The police didn't search his possessions?"

"When you think about it, why would they? What would they be looking for?"

"Sure... as you say. Why are you telling me this?"

Eve turned to me, and the taut skin on her face stretched in the infancy of a smile. "You need to know that I know."

"Know what? I mean, apart from who invited who to 'Pine Hill'."

"That you lied to the police and in all probability murdered my husband."

"I've said everything about that in my statement to the police, and I can't say any more."

"Oh, come on. If the police knew of your lie about Bucky's visit, they would have to reopen the investigation. You'd also be charged with trying to pervert the course of justice or obstructing the police or something like that."

"The conclusion would be the same. No case," I said with a boldness I didn't feel.

"No. You know it was a very close decision by the District Attorney. I know that. As a bereaved wife I had a full explanation from him in person. And I happen to know him. This lie, and it's a crucial lie, could start a prosecution."

I tried to sound firm. "What are you going to do?"

Eve sat quietly looking into space for perhaps thirty seconds, the longest thirty seconds of my life.

"Nothing...nothing... nothing," she breathed.

"Then why...?"

"It's cathartic I suppose. Seeing you. Letting you know what I know. Do you have any idea, have you ever thought how I feel?"

"I have. I felt sorry for you. Anybody married to him..."

"I don't want or need your sympathy. I've had to wade through a filthy bog, full of disgusting revelations, getting deeper and deeper. I know all the details of your story. Don't you think I followed this thing closely? My lawyers were talking to the police and the DA's office all the time. I happen to *know* you told a whole bundle of lies, including the most significant one of all, about the visit to the lake, so don't give me any bullshit."

"My version of events has been accepted as true," I said flatly.

She scoffed, "Your version of events has prevailed so far, that's all. It's never been accepted by the police."

"But you don't want me indicted..."

Eve raised her voice and showed distaste for the first time. "A trial? Do you think I would want a trial? I've already been spread over TV stations and newspapers from here to San Francisco by the inquest. I don't care about your lies. *I want it over, finished*!"

"Well, it is."

Eve stood up to go. "I'll tell you, that as a woman, I think I understand the position you were placed in. I don't know what I would have said or done myself."

She pointed to the tape-recorder and the diary on the couch. "Take those with you. Burn them, or keep them amongst your souvenirs."

Eve clasped her coat around her, looped her bag over her arm, and walked away with her head up. She snapped her fingers at a bell-man by the door, and casually held high the parking ticket for her car.

I sat on the couch for a while after Eve had gone, drained of strength. It happens that I had thought of her many times during my ordeal. I knew she had suffered. I had no idea how long she had been married to Chadwin, but his pursuit of me could not have been his first infidelity. I faintly admired the fact that she had remained mute about her feelings for Chadwin – but perhaps her silence said it all. She had endured the public humiliation of being married to a man whose raging sexual impulses took him to the edge of madness.

But it was all over, and *both* of us were free.